37 st

CH00866418

ty

Patricia Ace

The publisher acknowledges subsidy from the Scottish Arts Council towards
the publication of this volume

 Scottish
Arts Council

Published by Freight
49-53 Virginia Street
Glasgow
G1 1TS

ISBN 978-0-9544024-4-0

First published 2008

Copyright © Fiona Rintoul and Susan Kemp 2008
All rights reserved

A CIP catalogue record for this book is available from The British Library

Typeset in Archer.
Printed and bound in Great Britain by TJ International Ltd, Padstow, Cornwall.

Let's Pretend

37 stories about (in)fidelity

Edited by Susan Kemp and Fiona Rintoul

Published by Freight, Glasgow

Contents

Foreword

We're billing this collection of short stories by new writers as 'the book the Church of Scotland didn't want to print'. *Let's Pretend: 37 stories about (in)fidelity* is now in the warm and open-minded hands of Freight, but initially it was to be published by St Andrew Press, the Church of Scotland's publisher. We had concerns. Of course, we did. But they were vigorously allayed by St Andrew Press, who were at pains to emphasise their liberal mindedness. In fact, they seemed slightly insulted that we thought they might have a problem with, you know, those old demons – swearing, sex, and, erm (speak it not), *homosexuality.*

Then the manuscript arrived.

The rest, as they say, is history and need not detain us here. Suffice to say that we take great comfort from the words of the former Bishop of Edinburgh, Dr Richard Holloway, now chairman of the Joint Board of the Scottish Arts Council and Scottish Screen, who recently wrote in favour of 'creative disloyalty':

> *If creative irresponsibility often lies at the heart of genius, it is not a surprise that the artist is often afraid of being co-opted or controlled by authority. As [Graham] Greene has already warned us, we see the danger at its most blatant in totalitarian societies, where the artist is only allowed to produce art that conforms to the objectives of the State. We also see it in religious institutions, where artists are encouraged to conform their art to the values of the faith they follow.*

Try to recruit or civilise artists and you lose them, suggests Dr Holloway, and he is right. Hurrah for creative disloyalty! Art, literature, is about saying exactly what you like, exactly how you like. Attempts to tone things down to please a particular congregation are really censorship and must be resisted at all costs. Anyone who doesn't understand that has no business publishing literature. Or, as one of our esteemed authors put it, noting that the collection's theme is and always has been (in)fidelity, 'What the fuck did they think the stories were going to be about?'

The 37 stories in this collection all come from new writers currently taking the MLitt in Creative Writing at Glasgow University. *Let's Pretend* is but the latest offering from the Glasgow course, which has produced many excellent collections of new writing in the past, and it is the first to have a theme. We are very proud of the diverse and unabashed way that the writers have responded to the theme of (in)fidelity. It's all there – fornication, adultery, blasphemy, sodomy, witchcraft, even the odd bit of love and loyalty – and so it should be.

We live in a time when the pressure not to say certain things can sometimes be acute. *Please don't publish those cartoons again because they might upset people.* That kind of thing. But, in fact, we must always say everything we want to say. Because if *we* don't say it, who will? The story in this collection that provoked the most intense heebie-jeebies did so because characters in it said things about Islam and Judaism. But to take exception to such a story is to make the same simplistic mistake as those who persuaded Simon & Schuster, the company originally slated to publish Brett Easton Ellis's *American Psycho*, to drop it – the age-old one of shooting the messenger.

We are grateful to all the writers who contributed to this collection both for their diligence in responding to the theme, and for the imaginativeness and variety of their responses. We are also grateful to the tutors on the Glasgow University MLitt programme for the work they've done in bringing on the writers featured in *Let's Pretend*. Finally, we would like to offer our sincere thanks to Ian Rankin for kindly agreeing to introduce the book and to our enlightened publisher Freight, both for taking us on and for the excellent job they've done on the collection.

We hope you enjoy these 37 naughty, naughty stories, filled to the brim with sweary words and hochmagandy!

Susan Kemp and Fiona Rintoul
Glasgow, August 2008

Preface

Ian Rankin

My first success of any kind as a writer came with a poem.

I was seventeen and in my final year at high school. I entered the poem in a competition and came second. Emboldened, I went on to university as a poet but soon found myself with a problem – my poems were telling stories; they were not 'emotion recollected in tranquillity'. It wasn't long before I switched to writing short stories, and I relished the freedom. My characters suddenly had more room to breathe, and their complex inner lives could stretch further than a couplet or a verse. I couldn't understand why more people weren't publishing and reading short stories. They seemed to me the perfect literary form for our busy urbanised lives. Bus journey into town? A story would fill the time. Train to and from work? A story would see you there.

I started to devour collections of short stories. Jayne Anne Phillips was an early favourite, as was Ian McEwan. My own stories started out as five or six sides of paper. It seemed a real feat when one edged into double figures. But I had to start pruning when I submitted stories to BBC radio – the beeb had a daily slot of fifteen minutes, which meant a story of around five sides (1,500 words). Magazines and anthologies imposed their own rules and regulated lengths, but I liked a challenge. Even today, if a magazine stipulates that the story I send them should feature a deep-fried Mars Bar, a game of Cluedo, and Edinburgh Castle, it's hard to resist the lure.

The contributors to *Let's Pretend* were told to limit their stories to around 1,500 words. They were also warned that each submission should be on the theme of (in)fidelity – albeit interpreting the word as freely as imagination would allow. The resulting stories form as strong a collection as I've read in a decade or more. Wit and wistfulness, black skies and blue, laughter and tragedy – all are on display here. Celaen Chapman provides the title story; it fizzes with energy and radiates the heat of first love. C J Begg's tale contrasts a tender narrative with a disturbing narrator. 'Origami' by Kirsty Logan has a twisted logic all of its own, while Sean McLaughlin's story is about language itself and the struggle to make it say what we need it to say.

Oh, and one glance at C J Begg's opening sentence and you're guaranteed to read on.

The 37 writers here, all of them MLitt students on Glasgow University's Creative Writing programme, offer a compelling diversity of approaches, locations and styles. The tone can be confessional or objective, and religion underpins several of the narratives. Some are presented in English, others in Scots. There are affairs, assignations, promises kept and broken. Human failings and frailties are laid bare. But there is heroism, too, alongside reassuring shafts of humour. Each and every story has something to offer, and the collection as a whole rekindles my enthusiasm for the short story as a meaningful form, perhaps the most vitally immediate we have.

Stane flinger

Joe McInnes

I don't believe in God. In fact I hate his guts. If it wiznae for him ma Da would still be alive and ma Ma wouldnae be shagging the butcher. An don't try tae tell me it's no true cause I seen them with ma own eyes. Anyway, how else dae you explain all that butcher meat in oor fridge? No unless you think its some kinda miracle.

Miss Lucas the school counsellor says it's no a sin if you don't believe in God. She says it's jist natural for me tae be angry. But I telt Father Conn an he says it's a question of faith.

'Tell me something that frightens you, Connie?' he asked. 'It doesn't have to be anything big, just something that scares you a little.'

'Well I get absolutely terrified in English when Mr Campbell asks people tae read oot loud,' I telt him. If I'm honest I didnae have a clue what that had tae dae with ma Da dying.

But Father Conn rubbed his hauns an says, 'That's exactly the kind of thing I mean.'

Tae tell the truth I never thought nothing else aboot it till a few weeks later when Campbell's Meat Balls announces everybody in the class is tae write a story for a school project. 'I'll choose the best three and those selected will read their story at the school open day.'

I was paranoid cause I thought what I telt Father Conn was jist between me an him.

'One more thing,' says Meat Balls, putting his hauns up an hodden everybody back after the bell had went. 'The topic of your story has to be faith.'

I was pure raging an when I got oot the classroom marched straight along the corridor tae the R.E department. Father Conn was sitting behind his desk when I barged intae his office.

'Did you tell Mr Campbell I was too scared tae read oot in front the class?' I shouted.

'Connie, come in and take a seat for goodness sake.' He acted as if he was pure calm but you could see he was a bit taken aback. 'How's your Mum, we don't see much of her at Chapel these days?'

I ignored him an stood at the door an repeated what I'd said. 'Did you tell Mr Campbell I was too scared tae read oot in front of the class?'

'For heavens sake Connie will you come in and close the door and stop all this shenanigans?' He got up an came oor tae me an says for me tae sit doon.

He wiznae wearing his jacket an his priest collar was tied roon his back like ma wee brother Stephen's bib. He sat next tae me on the edge of the desk an began talken. I folded ma arms an pure stared at the picture of Saint Anthony on the wall behind him.

'I only suggested to Mr Campbell about organising a story competition. I never said a thing about you being afraid to read out in class,' he says. 'Why, what on earth's happened?'

'I suppose it was your brilliant idea tae make the story aboot faith?'

'I won't deny it,' he says. 'Anyway, why are you so upset? As far as I was led to believe only the best stories are to be read out.'

'Are you trying tae say ma story will no be good enough?' I glared at him.

'That's the spirit,' he says. 'And I think we both know you can do anything you set your mind on.'

'I couldnae read it oot though,' I says. 'I'd be petrified.'

'You just need a bit of faith,' he says.

'An jist where am I supposed tae find this faith?' I looked at him as if he could open his desk drawer an pull some oot.

'You'll have to wait until you read your story at the open day,' he says. 'That's faith's secret. You get it *after* you act.'

'How dae you know ma story will even get picked?' I asked, thinken I'd clamped him.

But he acted all holy like an says, 'Let's just say I've got faith in the script writer.'

Soon as I came in the close I could smell stewed sausages. On every landing the stink got stronger an by the time I stepped throu the front door I had tae hold ma nose. I went straight intae ma room grabbed the Impulse an sprayed it everywhere.

'Dinner's nearly ready,' Ma shouted.

'I'm no hungry,' I shouted back.

'You better bloody eat something girl,' she bawled.

'Bloody better eat something,' copied Stephen.

It'd been like this ever since ma Da died. If he'd been still alive we'd be having spaghetti hoops or else a tin of macaroni. But noo ma Ma can get her hauns on free butcher meat its stovies every single night.

'I'm no hungry,' I repeated.

'No hungry,' shouted Stephen.

'I'm warning you,' Ma persisted.

'Warning you,' says Stephen.

'Okay then,' I yelled. 'I'll have a wee drap potatoes an gravy if that'll make you happy.'

'Tatoes an gravy make you happy.'

After I finished ma dinner I went back tae ma room tae start work on ma story. But an oor later I was sitting sterren at a blank page cause every time I tried tae write aboot faith I kept thinken aboot ma Da having a heart attack. I flicked throu ma bible an found a bit that says even demons believed in Jesus an I felt like a pure hopeless case. After that I decided tae make up a pack a lies.

Aboot seven o'clock ma Ma stuck her heid roon the door. I kept on writing an she came intae the room an sat on the edge of the bed. She was wearing her favourite skirt, the black an white wan with the fluers an a black blouse you could see her bra throu.

'What are you writing?' she asked trying tae peek oor ma shoulder.

'We've tae write a story for a school project,' I answered, clutching the pad tae ma chest.

'Member that story you wrote aboot your holy communion? The *White Dress*,' she says. 'I showed it tae Father Conn an he says you were a natural.'

'How come you never go tae Chapel any merr?' I says. 'First when ma Da died you were always rushin aff tae see Father Conn.'

'You're too young tae understaun, Connie,' she says. 'Anyway, what I want tae ask – '

'Would you watch Stephen?' I says, mimicking her.

'Would you, hen?' she says. 'I've jist put him doon an that should be him for the nite.'

'As long as you don't bring your fancy man back here,' I says.

Last time I was baby sitting Stephen had fell asleep in ma bed. I woke up during the nite and carried him intae ma Ma's room an found her an her boyfriend on top of the bed bare naked. She knew what I was talken aboot cause she took a pure beamer.

'I've got needs like everybody else, Connie.'

'Too much information,' I says, an put ma hauns oor ma ears.

Who knows how ma crap story ever got picked cause I jist wrote a lot of garbage. But somedae must of been listnen tae Father Conn cause on the open day there I was staunen on the stage in the assembly hall with the whole school watchen.

Miss Lucas says I didnae have to read ma story if I didnae want tae. Then I saw ma Ma's boyfriend walk intae the hall with his wife. I was beeling, specially since I looked oor at ma Ma an she turned away kiddin on she never even seen him.

Campbell's Meat Balls introduced me an I walked tae the centre stage. I held ma story at ma side but I knew I wasnae going tae need it. When I talked intae the microphone I was totally calm.

I don't believe in God. In fact I hate his guts. If it wiznae for him my Da would still be alive and my Ma wouldnae be shagging the butcher. And don't try tae tell me it's no true cause I seen them with my own eyes. Anyway, how else dae you explain all that butcher meat in oor fridge? No unless you think its some kinda miracle.

After that it was pure chaos. The butcher's wife stood up and started calling ma Ma for everything. When the butcher tried to shut her up she tore intae him as well. I looked oor at ma Ma an she was slunk right doon in her seat. Stephen was on her knee an she was trying to hide behind him. She looked totally mortified. Meat Balls came up an dragged me aff the stage. The weirdest thing was Father Conn, who was staunen in the wings sterren doon at ma Ma an in his haun he was carrying a big massive stane.

Consequences

Adrian Searle

It's been a late one. As Callum locks up the restaurant he checks his watch: quarter to two.

When he reaches the gates to the grand house he parks his car and walks the half mile down the drive. He can't risk being mistaken for a thief. Although his eyes grow accustomed to the darkness, everything remains indistinct. The silhouettes of trees and bushes leak into dirty blackness.

When he arrives, the wooden door to the walled garden is locked. With a struggle he climbs the wall. As he hauls himself over the top he scrapes his knee, feels the stinging beneath his thin kitchen trousers.

He'd first arrived at the house five years before, only his second job after college. The building seemed impossibly large. He couldn't believe he'd ever master its geography; corridors leading to east and west wings, drawing rooms, dining rooms; narrow wooden stairs up to the servants' quarters, stone steps leading down to a warren of storerooms.

Kirsten, a chambermaid, showed him to his room. It was a good size with an old-fashioned iron bedstead and a ceiling that followed the slope of the roof. The girl was local, came from a village five miles away.

'I've worked in shops and spent a year looking after old folks,' she said. 'As jobs go, they were pretty rubbish. But I like it here.'

There was something about her that Callum liked. It was in her eyes.

He worked hard, learning from the head chef, an old Italian guy. In three months he and Kirsten were going to the pub together, taking it in turns to drive. At night, after they'd made love on the old bedstead, they'd lie together listening to the wind in the eaves. To Callum anything seemed possible.

On Sundays, if they both had the day off, they'd walk in the grounds. The house had pasture to the front and gardens at the sides and rear. There was a rose garden enclosed by high hedges and a Spanish garden with a pond full of goldfish, but they both liked the sculpture garden best. They'd sit in the summer house holding hands, listening to the finches in the cherry trees, and they'd enjoy looking at the statues. There were several classical busts – men in helmets and women with aquiline noses – and a collection of animals; a horse, a lion, a unicorn, a pig, a frog and a griffin – each representing a famous politician or diplomat, friends of the family before the First War, so the head chef said.

Callum and Kirsten preferred the statue of the small girl. She was tucked away in a corner, overgrown with ivy and green with lichen. She stood on a granite plinth, hands clasped together, looking out across the garden. No one knew who she was but there was something in the way she stood, the straightness of her back and tilt of her head, which fascinated them.

'I think she's been neglected,' Kirsten said one afternoon. 'We should ask if we can clean her up. I'm sure she'd like it.'

The estate manager didn't mind and over time they cut back the ivy, carefully scrubbed her clean, weeded the border at the base of the plinth and planted new flowers. It was something they did together, a project.

If Callum had time, even if Kirsten was working, he'd go and do what he could: tidy up, remove debris that collected in the corner, pull out any weeds. He missed his girlfriend's company so he talked to the statue as he worked. He'd tell her about his day, about the people he worked with in the house and about the guests that paid to come and stay. He described new recipes, interesting ingredients he'd discovered. And he talked about Kirsten.

Callum liked the time he spent there. It was quiet, the wind gentle. His mind felt clearer when he was alone with the statue of the little girl. Life made more sense.

Within a year of getting married, Callum knew he'd made a mistake. He and Kirsten disagreed over a shopping trip and she sulked for two days. She insisted they take holidays he couldn't afford. She wouldn't visit his parents, said they didn't like her. She stopped going to the pub. She fell out with the housekeeper and then spent two weeks sick in bed. His dissatisfaction was small at first, so insignificant it might have been overlooked, but soon his life became ruled by her little tyrannies.

When he could, he walked down to the sculpture garden and sat with the stone girl.

They needed more money, so he found a better job at a restaurant. The head chef was sorry to lose him. The hours at the restaurant were long; it took him months to get used to starting at eleven and finishing well into the small hours. Kirsten began at seven so they saw little of each other. Her moods grew darker and the time they did spend together was filled with all the things they couldn't say.

Julie, a waitress, joined the restaurant six weeks after him. He enjoyed chatting to her on his break. She confided in him. Over time, in those moments when she thought no one was watching, he saw something in her that he recognised in himself: disappointment. If he looked closely enough it was there, like the tiny patterns of cracked glaze on the antique crockery he used to work with every day.

He told the statue about her, the things they discussed at the back door of the kitchen, her problems at home. As always, the girl on the plinth understood.

He'd always remember the midnight cold the night he left the grand house, the moon high in the sky. Standing there looking up at the tiny attic, light still raging from the window.

The owners were kind. They rented him a small cottage on the far side of the estate and he promised some extra help in return. Then Julie moved in.

A week later he arranged to collect his remaining possessions; clothes, books, photographs, CDs. When Kirsten opened the door of the attic room, Callum saw she'd lost weight – he knew he had – and her eyes were dark with shadow. She said nothing as he packed his things. To Callum, everything about the room seemed smaller. It was as if it had all shrunk; the walls, the ceiling, the furniture, even Kirsten. As he carried the last of the boxes to the car she appeared outside.

'I don't want you visiting the garden again,' she said. 'Leave me that, at least.'

He was taken by surprise, didn't know what to say.

'But I've spent much more time looking after her,' he said. 'You know I have. I can't just stop.'

'She was always mine. It was my idea, for God's sake.' The pitch of her voice was rising.

'It was something we did together.'

'Well, we're not together any more.' She paused. 'Don't be difficult. You know I need her more than you.'

And then she walked back inside, closing the door behind her.

As the months passed, living with Julie, Callum realised how unhappy he'd been. Now life was simple, enjoyable. He was in love. But he couldn't forget the girl in the sculpture garden. As he cut vegetables in the kitchen he thought about her. At night he dreamed he was in the garden again, weeding, cutting back the ivy, talking to the statue.

One Saturday afternoon, he returned to the grand house. As he walked down the narrow path between the gardens he could feel his chest tightening, the excitement of seeing the statue mixed with the fear of meeting Kirsten.

She was sitting there, in the sculpture garden, reading a book. The bench was new; it'd been placed in the corner, next to the stone girl, like a sentry box. The statue stood as she always had, back straight and hands clasped, looking out at him.

Kirsten stared.

'Why are you here?' she said.

'I want to see her.'

'You can't.'

'Why not?' he said.

'Because I don't want you to. Because she's mine.'

'But I need to see her,' he said.

'I won't let you,' said Kirsten.

Callum drops to the ground, his boots making a muffled thump on the wet grass. Inside the sculpture garden it seems even darker, but slowly shapes emerge; a helmet, the profile of a horse. He looks up, catches the briefest glimpse of stars through a gap in the clouds, then reaches down and touches his knee. There's a damp patch and he can feel a small hole where he's ripped his trousers. With soft footsteps he crosses to where he knows the statue of the girl should be.

In the corner, surrounded by ivy, it's impossible to see her shape. He feels consumed by darkness. He puts out a hand, reaching for the plinth. A few steps forward and he finds it. Callum knows he has left this moment too long, that time has opened like a crevasse between them. He should have fought harder, stood up to Kirsten from the start. The stone feels so cold against his palm. And at that moment he knows the spell is broken, that the stone girl is no longer his.

Refusal

Roy McGregor

When leaving our house I saw your phone sitting on the hall table. It wasn't a deal of any sort. I thought that you might have needed it. For what though? To call me? But you never did that when you were away. Had there been distance in your eyes when you looked at me that I saw but didn't register? Was there some suspicion in my thoughts when I called your hotel? I can't say that there was. But somewhere on the borders of my imagination, on the ragged edge of my thoughts, I think of you as someone I have never known and could never possibly know were I to be with you a thousand years. I feel as though I were caught clumsily in a turnstile of emotion. I think so much about you and I think equally about myself, but I never think of others. To give thought to others would be to give them some credence in this sorry state of affairs. It would be to give them life and a sense of substance; something I cannot do, something perhaps I will not do. The reality that I wanted to hold on to was inhabited by just two people. Then something was dragged into that ideal, some obscene essence was brought to my door. It was you that did that.

For you to have come to me would have given me some crumbs of respect. For you to have come to me and spoken to me would have given me something to cling to; I would have felt less bereft, or indeed bereaved. You gave me nothing, no words, no tears, no tenderness. If there had been some small signal that would have prepared me I truly would have held on to it. That much would have given me a modicum of understanding. But that's not how it was. I saw nothing, I suspected nothing because you kept your life from me. That's clear to me now. How else could you have conducted such a betrayal?

Like our love affair your betrayal of me was somehow just as pure within its own shabby construction. It was only on the moment of discovery that both fell, not like a colossus, but so much less. And that was part of my surprise, that the sun would go down at dusk and rise again. For my bliss to stop I thought would stop the world on its axis. Every move would be stilled and every tongue dumbed. It was not a wild romantic notion, for that euphoric state that I held myself in seemed to be everything, it was my *raison d'être*, my breath and heartbeat. How could I have imagined your feelings less? How could I imagine you being less than that?

I drove to the station and waited for your train to arrive. While I waited I thought of the embarrassed desk clerk. I, who would let no one intrude on us, let this bit player enter. He could not imagine the part he would play in our lives. He entered from the shadows. He told me that you were with another man. He had described you and it could only have been you. By the time he realised the significance of his words it was too late. And he left as he arrived, a disembodied voice, now left somewhere in the ether of my thoughts.

I had many things to say, but it was you that I wanted to hear. I wanted to know where any of this started. When did you first think so little of me? And then in the blurred group of travellers I saw you. You appeared radiant and beautiful. An angel. More than you had for such a long time. Is this what infidelity brings? Radiance? Beatitude?

I took your bag from you and nodded towards the station café. I walked and you walked by my side. The woman behind the counter also looked betrayed; her face pale with a red gash mouth. Or maybe she looked like death. When I see such people I think that we have been so lucky. So lucky to have had what we have had.

As we moved towards a table a cliché formed in my head: do we have a future together? I dismissed that immediately but it was what I wanted to say. I carried your tea and sat beside you at the table you had chosen. It was filthy. Spilled tea, coffee and sugar stained the top. Crushed up napkins, used and wet with the cold fluids. I didn't care. I didn't care because it reflected the mess that you had brought to my life. How the other customers must have viewed us I can only guess. We didn't belong there, that much was clear.

I can't read your face. You sit opposite me and I can't read your face. And I have been with you so long. But now I don't know what it is I'm seeing. Is it your shock at having been caught and faced with the shabbiness of it all?

Are you trying to answer as to why any of this came about? Or do you know the answer and are struggling with the truth about us? I cannot tell anything any more. I thought I knew your very soul. In truth, I understand now, I knew absolutely nothing. And that's as big a shock to me as anything else. Did I take you for granted? Is that what it means to trust?

You can't even look at me. Is that a matter of shame? Or is it something else altogether? Your head comes up and your lips part as though you are about to speak. Go on, I think, say it. But words don't come from your mouth. Nothing at all comes from your mouth. You are locked into silence. But that doesn't last. And what issues forth is a surprise.

You giggle. Not a girlish or coquettish giggle, but a mature woman's giggle. A sound that seems to say, *Oops*. Yes, that's it, *Oops, I've just been unfaithful*. This catches me, for in some region of my mind I must have been expecting something else, almost anything else. I am wrong-footed. What an original woman you are. What a wonderfully original human being you are. The expected would have been tears, a certain amount of pleading, a gesture of remorse. But a giggle? And it doesn't stop there. It carries on and becomes a laugh. Your hand goes up to your face and I see that you have lost control. It crosses my mind that nervous laughter at funerals is not uncommon. The emotions are often confused by grief and the wrong one is brought to the graveside. But it is not that. There is not confusion here. You are now laughing because you find this whole situation funny. You find it funny that you have been caught red-handed, and you find it funny that you woke up this morning beside another man.

And then you do look at me, with tears falling from your eyes. The back of your hand is brushed across your cheeks and I feel foolish. Just foolish. Foolish to have been treated in such a way and foolish to react as I did.

And now I join you. How could I do otherwise? Other tables' eyes have settled and smile on us. They think that we're crazy old lovers, madly and hotly in love. And we laugh and hold each other's hands. I pull my hand from you and make the mime of a gun at my head and that sets us off again wildly. You are screaming now and stamping your feet on the floor. I remember years ago you peed yourself laughing at my jokes. It came through your knickers and tights and splashed on to the pavement, my wonderful mad-as-snakes girl. And others have joined in with the laughter now, even the grim reaper behind the counter, laughing as though she had just this moment discovered the ability to do so. You point to her and whoop loudly and then hold your sides. I want to say something but there is nothing to say; anything spoken might end it. It is all we can do to gather breath between the laughter.

We will soon rise from the table and still in hysterics, no doubt, leave the café and leave the station. We will drive home and close the door on the whole of the wide world. And you will be new to me again. Bringing back a stranger from the borders and ragged edges. Bringing you to my core. And that's where I need you. At the centre of me. And I will turn away from anything that denies my being with you. I will refuse to let enter anything that denies me you.

Birds in the back lane

Jenni Brooks

Time has slowed down. Their tattooed arms are frozen, bulging, entwined. Big Joe's in trouble. Every warm welcome, every victory, plays across his mind in a slow silent movie. Every slap on the back, every yard of ale given in ceremony and downed to raucous applause. His head spins with trophies, his repeating name filling their shiny plaques. First it'd been local pubs around Mitcham; as word had spread he was asked to matches further afield, gradually spanning out across south London. It was only when he'd crossed the river that he realised something remarkable was happening. He had started to exist.

Funny things happened if you were good at something. People knew who he was, they gave him things. They respected him. After one fixture The *Croyden Star* said he had the stature of a working class warrior. He liked that. He'd always been solid (his ma used to say *built like a brick shithouse*) but never had the mouth to match. His size had made him awkward and quiet, he'd left school early and kept his head down. He was never going to come to much. That is, until the first arm wrestle he got goaded into one October afternoon in Tatchell's pub – the day when everything changed. In the years that followed, Big Joe didn't waste any time getting into role. Victory followed victory, in the small then big leagues, local then national. In those days television was still a family pastime for special occasions, and pubs still men's places. Places of sawdust and blood and loyalty. He grew to see the whole of London and the south-east as his own, one vast arena of combat and glory. Willy his manager steered his course every step, setting up promos and challenge matches wherever he could. Big Joe's name on the handbills was guaranteed to draw the crowds. Joe was tireless in those days – batting off all comers like a bull swishing flies away with his tail. He scarcely blinked.

He's still invincible, still winning. But these last few months Willy's no-ticed the match times creeping up. Not that the big man ever looks in bother, he just seems to be taking longer to go for the kill. A trickle of sweat snakes its way down Joe's stocky back. He bluffs, but he's in a bad way. They've been locked for twenty minutes and Joe's opponent shows no signs of tir-ing. Finton's stringy fingers have been white for most of that time, yet his grip never falters. The air throbs thick around them. Big Joe swallows dryly, Adam's apple rasping in his constricting throat. The time has finally come. Go on big guy, it's now or never. He'd always known about other ways to win, but sailed through on talent alone. But lately Joe's been leaving the nail on his little finger longer, knowing sooner or later his rep would be on the line. He's been treating the nail with horsetail to toughen and harden it, every morning and again in the back house before bedtime. Some filing at the edges too, to craft a small, lethal, razor point at its centre. Joe's nurtured the nail as though it was one of his beloved pigeons; it's become a protective talisman. The self-made weapon's well positioned so no-one will ever know. He's snagged it on his shirt a few times and once the cloth tore. He didn't have to lie giving it to the wife to mend – I caught it on a nail, he said. She knows what's going on anyway, but would never say anything. She fears for him once the wrestling stops – a time which, she senses, can't be far away. His once calm, long nights are now shot through with fractious dreams. He never speaks of them, but he writhes beside her where before he'd laid like a log, and he looks grey and empty across the morning table.

Big Joe summons all worldly will into the little finger of his rigid hand. He grits his jaw; with an audible exhalation he gouges the piercing nail deep into Finton's clammy flesh. He waits, staring, for the pain to penetrate. But Finton doesn't move. He doesn't flinch. Not a flicker passes over his face.

Fixing his eyes on Joe, Finton smiles inside as a spike of pain shoots up his prickly forearm. So, the wily old bugger's putting the nail in. Sure enough, he's heard of the sorts of tricks the old guys get up to, but this is the first sign of it in his short fast rise on the scene. He'd dismissed nailing as one of the many myths that get spun, especially to incomers like himself. But there's no doubting it. This god of wrestlers – the one he's heard lauded since his very first match, the unconquered hero, this boulder of a man filling up his face – is cheating. Joe's sour, metallic breath steams into his skin. Without breaking the eye lock between them, Finton gathers a sticky globule of sputum in his mouth and flobs it to the floor. So, that's how the champ's going to play it. Finton knows he can end it, all he need do is nod at the official, have a word and it'll be over. Big Joe would be destroyed at a stroke and the title his. But he doesn't. He sits tight, does nothing. The pain is sharp but not excruciating – he's stomached a lot worse. His old fighting coach used to rib him for his high pain threshold and seemed to enjoy testing it. Boxing had kept him in ale and more for a few years, mind, and the alley stuff came in handy when he needed extra cash. No, he doesn't bother about a few cuts and bruises here and there, he can take a beating. Though he stews sometimes about the pain thing; one dark morning last year rather than springing out of bed like normal, he hadn't been able to move a muscle. In that chilling instant, flat on his back, he knew what real pain was. It turned out it was living deep inside him – an insistent treacle of pain which leaked from his bones now and then and came bubbling up, screaming, to the surface. So the sitting sport's the better bet for his future now, he knows that – it's easier than the fist fights and will reap plenty cash in due course too. Yet still he doesn't end it. There's something about Joe's pale eyes which stops Finton dead. He smells the old man's bitter breath getting stronger with every gasp. And then he sees it – a dim streak of terror fleets across Joe's spent face. It's distasteful, mortifying, to see his revered opponent fade like this. Nothing's worth that, he thinks – sad old bugger. It's only a bit of Sunday fun, at the end of the day.

Big Joe's broken. If the nail's failed, then he has – he's got nothing left to fight with. It's over, he's falling. He doesn't know what to do – he doesn't lose, he doesn't know how. He longs to be at home – at his table or down the back lane with his birds. Perhaps he could bear it there, but not here – he can't still be here. How's it going to end? He'd do anything to fast forward to a place he feels safe again. He must let go, but he can't. He can't unclench his muscles, which have hardened against him like setting cement. He'll fall into a thousand pieces the moment he tries to stand. And still time stretches on. He wants to end it, but can't even do that. But suddenly, like a dam breaking, the tension shatters. That's it. It's really over.

Their arms fall to the side. Big Joe's head swings back on his shoulders. Salty sweat seeps into his fisted eyes. He feels the crowd pull him to his feet. The jostling sounds around him are distant and muddled, then Willy's voice cuts through.

'You had me worried there for a minute, you old bugger!'

Joe's eyes open slowly. Everything blurs. He blinks. Amid diffused halos of light, he's sure he sees smiles. He looks into his manager's face, uncomprehending.

'You've won Joe. It's ours! My boy's still the champ!'

Big Joe's loyal crew hoist his lumpen frame up to the rafters. Ecstasy courses his body. He's where he should be, has to be – the place that's rightfully his. He'd always said to himself, the minute I need the nail, that's it. No more. And what better way to go than as undefeated champion? But the nail is long forgotten. This is what's real.

'Maybe there's another season in you after all!'

A tankard's shoved into his hand, foam sloshing over the top. He takes a deep, syrupy swig. Out of a sea of soft handshakes one steel grip stiffens him. Finton glistens at him like a ghost and pulls Joe close.

'I would've beaten you, mate, but I couldn't be bothered.'

Joe's hand withers in Finton's grip.

'You didn't beat me though, did you?' he blurts as he pulls away, reeling. Wiping froth from his ashen face he thinks to himself, one more season.

Truth be told

Sue Reid Sexton

Josie and Kath were tiring of the heat. Even in the shade of the big beech tree at the bottom of the garden the temperature was unbearable. Josie had rolled the bottom of her vest-top up under her lardy boobs. She waved a magazine at her belly but sweat continued to drip and stick in the creases of her love handles. Kath, she noticed, had dark stripes in the armpits of her grey T-shirt, and along the lines of her ribs and elsewhere.

Christina was not tiring of the heat. Josie watched her swaying, as usual, hands on her waist, in the middle of the lawn, with the regularity of the pendulum in the grandfather clock in the hall. Christina was dressed in khaki shorts, a matching vest like Josie's own, sagging over a teenage bosom, and rugged mountain boots. Dark hair fanned out in her armpits. It was the same colour as the long hair on her head which swung down her back in time to the movement of her legs. She was staring hard at the treetops.

'Come into the shade, darling,' Josie called.

Christina swayed on, left and then right, each foot slightly off the ground at the moment of return. Occasionally she hummed a little tune or muttered to herself. Josie sighed.

'We've got fresh lemonade from the fridge, the special stuff you like from Sparways,' she said.

But all to no avail.

'Come on,' Josie sighed again. There would be tantrums and sickness later, but then it would be cooler later too and she'd feel more able to deal with it.

'Come into the shade, darling,' said Christina to no-one in particular, but in Josie's own particular tones.

'Damn,' said Josie. 'I hate it when she starts that. Makes me feel like such a fool.' And she mimicked herself saying it again. 'Come into the shade, darling.'

'Come into the shade, darling,' said Christina in the middle of the lawn in the new exaggerated style.

'Oh God!' said Josie under her breath.

Kath started to laugh. 'But it must be funny sometimes, surely?' she said, dabbing at her forehead with a paper napkin. 'When she copies you I mean? Especially when there're guests about and they don't expect it?'

'Well, obviously,' said Josie, distracted, 'but not in this heat.'

'Postman's here!' said Christina, rocking. Then, 'Oh!' in a sudden shocked squeal.

'What is it?' said Kath, worried. She sat forward in the stripy deck chair.

'Nothing,' said Josie, and she closed her eyes for a moment. 'She means this morning.'

'She's very good at sounding like you. Very. What did you get this morning?'

'Nothing.'

'Oh, come on. Something from John?'

'God, how do birds manage to sing in this heat?'

'Josie...?'

'Mind your own business,' said Josie, fanning herself extra hard with a *Hello* magazine. The canvas beneath her made a farting noise as she reached for more lemonade. 'You know, you don't have to stay in this God awful heat. I'm used to John being away now. You can go home if you like.'

'But you always cry for the first three days.'

'Do I? No, I don't.'

'Josie...! And I always stay all day. It's what we do.'

'Is it?'

'Let's go back to bed,' said Christina, who had stopped temporarily on her right leg, waiting for the momentum to return, her left leg about a foot off the ground.

Josie glared at Christina. Christina stared up at the trees and swung back to her left, her dark, ratty tresses flaring over her shoulder. Josie felt Kath's eyes on her. She bumped her glass onto the metal table.

'Pour me another glass, will you?' she said, though her glass was still full.

'Come into the shade, darling.'

'Come into the shade, darling,' said Christina, swinging back to the right.

'Oh God!' said Josie.

'You're lucky you know when John's coming back,' said Kath. 'Robbie never knows 'til the last minute.'

'Really?' Josie glanced at Christina.

'You know it's true,' said Kath. 'I've told you that many times.'

'You know it's true,' said Christina, and Kath laughed, thrilled to be mimicked.

'I love it when she does it to me!' she said.

'Really?' said Josie.

'You know it's true,' said Christina to the beech tree, and Kath and Josie both laughed.

'Sounds just like me,' said Kath. 'Isn't she so clever? Who's a clever girl, then?'

'She's not a parrot, you know,' said Josie, tightly, 'or a baby. She's ill.' She felt her smile twitch. 'It's an illness,' she added flatly and she pushed back against her chair again.

'Sorry, Josie,' said Kath, drumming her fingers on the deckchair. 'But you have to see the funny side sometimes. I don't know how you cope. I'm sure I wouldn't. I'd have cracked up long ago and run off with a neighbour.'

Josie coughed, spilling some lemonade on to her shorts.

'Who would you go for?' she stammered, swatting at the dark patch with her damp fingers.

'Kath won't know,' said Christina in a deep voice.

'Who...?' said Josie. The word came out like a dog barking. 'Who would you go for? In the street I mean.'

'Well, give me a moment to think.' Kath's fingers rippled along her top lip.

'Ssh, you'll waken Christina,' hissed Christina.

'Come into the shade, darling! Now!' shouted Josie, making to stand up, the canvas groaning beneath her.

'Come into the shade, darling,' said Christina in Josie's exaggerated tones from earlier, then she added in a loud whisper, 'Not here, you gorgeous thing. Ssh, you'll waken Christina.'

Kath birled round to face her. She sat up straight in her deck chair, legs apart. Christina's swing had widened so that her left foot was two feet off the ground.

Josie closed her eyes hard and pushed back against the canvas.

'Well, what have you two love birds been up to?' said Kath in delight. 'Being away from each other must be good for you.' A pause. 'Josie? I said separation must be good for you, makes the heart beat faster or something.'

Josie's eyes were shut tight.

'Ooh, that's a good girl,' said Christina deeply, landing heavily on her left foot, the right surging upwards.

Josie's eyes flew open.

'She's not as good at your John,' said Kath.

'God, it's hot,' said Josie. 'Let's go in. She'll be all right out here.' She picked up the Hello magazine and started to fan herself again.

'But this is so interesting, Josie darling,' said Kath. 'I'm learning a lot!'

'God, you're hot!' growled Christina. 'Ooh, that's a good girl.'

'Well,' said Josie, trying to laugh, 'John's not here to defend himself, so I think we should...'

'Doesn't sound like he wants to defend himself,' said Kath. 'Lucky you!'

'Let's go indoors,' said Josie and she stood up, a trickle of sweat running down the dip that was her spine. Her glass tinkled against the jug on the table.

'Let me in, baby!' groaned Christina, legs apart, swinging almost at right angles.

'Goodness!' said Kath, chuckling.

'Come into the house, Christina! Now! This instant!' said Josie, striding towards her.

'I don't know what you're so embarrassed about,' said Kath. 'Wish my Robbie would say that stuff to me.'

'She's going to fall,' said Josie. Christina's leg was swinging back to earth.

'Come to think of it, it's exactly what he used to say...'

'Let me in Baby!' said Christina, as her leg landed heavily on the grass.

'Ha ha, yes, just like that,' said Kath. 'She's not very good at doing John though, is she?'

'Go to your room, Christina!' said Josie.

'Go to your room, Christina!' said Christina.

Christina's left leg was now at a full right angle to the ground. Josie put the ball of her fat hand on the heel of Christina's boot and pushed it just enough for Christina to lose her balance. She kept her own bulk between herself and Kath as she did so and stared hard into her daughter's eyes as she went down.

'Oh!' said Christina as she landed, in the same shocked squeal as before.

'Oh dear!' said Josie, and laughed lightly. 'Too late!' She waved to Kath. Kath's smile seemed to droop uncertainly, but she waved back.

Then 'Oh,' said Christina in a darker voice, 'that's good, Josie!' and she rolled on to her back, legs, arms and hair all spread-eagled on the grass.

'Much more like my Robbie,' said Kath. 'What a clever girl! Is she all right?'

Let's pretend

Celaen Chapman

It's Tuesday, 24th of May, 1988.

It's nearly time to walk the plank.

I'm standing barefoot on the headmaster's carpet.

I'm Anne Bonny facing the navy.

He's wearing a blue jacket with gold buttons.

I'm deliberately slovenly. I've got the prop cupboard sword tucked into my belt and there are moths crawling through the lining of my good woollen overcoat. My pockets are full of all the shiny things I've stolen for you; beads, sequins, pieces of coloured glass, compasses, penknives and blue marbles. I've got handcuffs tucked up inside my sleeve for you, taken from a policeman's daughter. She brought them here to show them off, the sun blinked and they glittered, I'm saving them for later because I know you'll love them. Last night you gave me a crimson feather, for luck, you said, and it still smells of you, of cedar wood, and your dark hair, and sleep, and me. I'm running it under my nose, twirling it between my fingers, looking him in the eye, thinking of you.

He has the storm coloured eyes of a reiver. He's jealous. All he can think about is how to plunder me.

Yesterday afternoon, after biology, after osmosis, when the sun was setting, he saw me kiss you under the rowan trees, (a real pirate kiss), and he watched us until you opened your eyes and looked at him, shifted into the sun and dazzled him, tricked the light and got away with it.

He ordered me to meet him here, just after sunrise on the second day of the week.

His office is like a cabin, high up, with a good view of the sky, the gathering clouds and the horizon. He has a barometer on the wall, but he hasn't strapped the books into his shelves, one swell and a pitch, and they'll all fall out, over us. Some of his books look very heavy. He has a tank filled with green water and the fish inside it are from tropical seas, the surface ripples when the wind buffets his windows. He's leaning towards me with his fingertips pressed into the wood of his desk. His fingers are too big; there's too much blood in them, as if his heart is leaking, and he has a quiet voice. He's talking about inappropriate and indecent behaviour.

He tells me that he's going to suspend me for a week. He says: after that, if you come back, and you tell me it's still real, the two of you, it would put me in a very difficult position.

He'd love to be put in a difficult position by us, I know he would. We'd cuff his hands and bind his ankles; we'd carry him through the neon corridors to our own dark cabin under the stage. We'd squeeze him between crates and costumes. We'd suspend him from the joists with ships rope. We'd paint green glitter above his eyes, coral-coloured lipstick on his lips, we'd sew strips of yellow silk into his hair and tickle him with feathers. Then we'd leave him, wrapped in a satin sail cloth, with a bottle of rum he couldn't reach, and if he's lucky, someone will find him in the morning, when the sun rises over the sea.

You're in a position of responsibility, he says.

This is an all girls' school. You're in sixth year. You have influence over people younger than you.

I would be in breach of the law, he says, if I didn't do this.

I look insolent and murderous.

I put my hand to the hilt of my sword. I want to challenge him to a duel and then slice all the gold buttons from his jacket without making the slightest scratch on his skin. I would rescue his fish, steal his books and sail away with you in a beautiful mahogany sloop, with twenty cannons pointing back at him, all the way to the horizon, just to make sure.

Listen, he says, and he tells me you've been offered a place to do drama at Cambridge, the only one from this school in ten years. And he says: if you carry on, you'll mess it up for her. It's such an opportunity, Cambridge.

A moth flies out of my coat, crosses over his desk and lands on his ear. He doesn't move.

Yes, I say, they have balls in Cambridge.

He looks at me. His fingertips have turned white.

I don't mean bollocks, I say, I mean dances. Sequins. Feathers. Rich pickings. I'll go with her.

And I look at him, smile, grin, show him my blacked out pirate teeth.

He says: You're not listening to me.

And I'm not, I'm thinking about how you turned me into a pirate.

I could tell him how you did it; it would torture him, it would haul him under the keel and drown him, for sure.

You dazzled me.

You were singing with your hands on your hips. You had amazonite in your ears and crimson feathers in your hair; you were wearing a sequin dress and a garnet necklace. You glittered.

I was standing on the balcony in my steel-tipped sea boots, lighting you up on the closing night, and when you looked up, just for a second, over a full house, through the light, and straight at me, I blushed. After the curtain calls and the applause, after he had given you a bouquet of roses and the lights went down, after he got into his car and drove home, you climbed onto a crate underneath the stage and waited. You didn't get changed and you didn't remove your make up. You sat cross-legged in the dark, the star of the show, waiting for me.

You watched me unwind the electrical cord from my shoulder and put the light on the floor. I didn't see you until you said:

If a skeleton walked into a bar what would it ask for?

Your voice was quiet and clear.

A pint of ale and a mop, I said, I know that one.

And I smiled and laughed anyway, and you tilted your head to one side, smiling back, looking at me from a different angle. Then you leaned forward and said, out loud, in the dark, that you wanted to kiss me.

I want to kiss you, you said.

And I pretended for as long as I could that I hadn't heard you, until you jumped down from the crate, took my hand and pulled me, tripping over the spotlight, into the prop cupboard. You switched the light off and closed the door.

You said: there could be a hundred spiders in here, eight hundred eyes watching us. You were a finger's width away, shimmering in the dark, a perfect spectre with the eyes of an otter.

Eight hundred wolf spider legs, you said, crawling all over you, and you kissed me and made spiders with your hands.

Then you leaned back, switched the light on, smiled at me again.

I wonder what you're going to do next? you said.

I switched the light off. You locked the door.

And we stayed until the building was completely silent. Until the hatches were battened and the moon came in through the windows, through the holes in the floorboards, and made flecks on us from a thousand miles away, you said.

We lay on a pile of soldiers' uniforms, your fingers through my fingers, surrounded by old fur coats and cardboard seas, you glimmered and glinted and you said: Let's pretend: I'm on a beach, I'm shipwrecked, I've been tipped off the deck of a 1930s Rotterdam to New York Liner, I'm cold and I'm lying under a round moon that's shining so gluttonously it's swallowed half of the stars.

You leaned over me.

You smoothed my eyebrows with your thumb.

You undid my buttons, one by one.

You said: Pretend you're a Pirate. You've got eyes like a pole cat, you could kill rabbits with your teeth and mesmerise sea eagles out of the sky. You anchor your ship at a moss-covered island and you sleep in a Viking house that's lit by candles and lined with bones. You have more riches than the stomach of a fish and you smear yourself with turtle blood to frighten the navy. You have herring in your bones and you eat limpet pie with your fingers.

You kissed my fingers.

You could suck out my spinal cord if you wanted to, you said.

You could muzzle me under the aurora borealis and throw me from the headland into the swell of the sea, if you wanted to.

You're a magpie, and I'm a trick of the light.

Pretend you've just found me washed up on your shore.

Pretend to take pity on me.

Pretend to fall in love with me, you said.

And I did.

'A local authority shall not... promote the teaching in any maintained school of the acceptability of homosexuality as a pretended family relationship.'

Section 28 of the Local Government Act 1986
Enacted 24 May 1988, repealed (Scotland) 21 June 2000

Well fucked and cherished

Patricia Ace

It is a weekday, a Tuesday, your son is at school and your husband is at work. You work part-time, but you don't work on a Tuesday. You hardly slept last night, snatched a few restless hours between one and four. Because today you have a meeting. You've arranged for one of the other mothers to pick up your son from school and look after him until six o'clock. That should give you enough time. Her son and your son are in the same class. They are friends. They are having a play date. You have a date of your own. An assignation. A tryst. Twelve o'clock at the train station in a town neither you nor he has any connection with. You've chosen the train station for practical reasons, even though you'll both be driving, but all the same the romance of it doesn't escape you. High Noon, he said on the phone. Sounds like we have a plan, you said.

It isn't the first time you've met. That was a while ago, at a book launch in the city. You got on well, spent most of the evening talking together, getting drunk, maintaining eye contact. You exchanged addresses, postal and email, so you could keep in touch, share your views on books and writing, strictly work-related. He mentioned that he shared his email address with his wife and you understood. *Don't worry, I'm not a bunny boiler or anything*, you said.

Everyone around you seemed to realise what was happening before you did. *Are you in love with him?* your friend asked on the drive home. Until that point, it simply hadn't occurred to you that you could fall in love with someone other than your husband. You'd been married for six years, were settled, believed you were happy. But recently you'd noticed that the affection you felt towards your husband was more like the love you feel for a sibling. You'd become aware of other men – at work, in the supermarket, even the occasional brave soul at the school gates. It was as if some kind of radar had suddenly been switched on. When you mentioned it to your friend, she called it the seven year itch. *Trust you to get it early,* she said. You'd always been precocious, premature. Maybe that's why you'd got married so young.

Your sex life hadn't been the same since your son was born five years ago. You had a vague troubling awareness that other people expected you to be trying for a second child. But neither you nor your husband has ever brought it up.

Are you in love with him? your friend asked on the drive home from the city, after the book launch. *He's obviously in love with you,* she said.

One or two letters were exchanged, but quickly deemed too risky. A few coded emails passed between you, then texts and eventually phone calls, strictly on mobiles. *I love your voice,* he said. Geographical distance kept you physically apart but the longing increased. The drive to meet again was irrepressible. And then an opportunity arose. He was going to be on a job in your neck of the woods, he was coming to the mainland. You just wanted to check that what you were feeling was real. You'd spent only five hours together and now you were in love. It seemed unlikely, impossible, as if you'd just made it up. But you couldn't ignore the signs. You'd lost weight, you'd become a raging insomniac, you'd started writing poetry again.

Your husband noticed the change in you too. *Are those new jeans you're wearing?* he said. *You look good – you're glowing.* You put it down to going to the gym more often (true) and the fact that you were feeling happier at work (a lie).

It's real. As soon as you see him at the station, your heart explodes. Your solar plexus feels like a gaping wound, all your senses on high alert. It's like being on acid – all the colours seem brighter, clearer; you're wide-eyed and speechless. You go to the cemetery and sit on a bench. You try to eat the picnic you've brought but neither of you has much of an appetite. It's cold and he is chittering so you give him your jacket to wear. It's brown velvet with large lapels. He looks like a real poet in it. *I bet you could really look after me,* he says. *Let me look after you,* you say.

You show each other photos of your spouses. You stare at a passport photo of his wife. Her face is strong, her expression intense, unsmiling. She looks like those photos of pioneering women in the American West. She looks nothing like you. *Very dramatic,* you say, meaning scary. He studies the photo you've given him. *He looks like a Viking,* he says. You smile a little at the thought of your husband as a Scandinavian marauder.

You go to a café to warm up. You order coffee and cake but again the food defeats you. He shows you a poem he has written. *It's about a mystical experience,* he says. He says he'd thought about booking a room, so that the two of you could talk in private. You already know he doesn't sleep in the same bed as his wife. *Perhaps you're just not into sex,* you say. *Oh, Daisy, you have no idea,* he says. He tells you he has this fantasy about you writing things on him. *I think women should be well-fucked and cherished,* he says. You couldn't agree more. You leave the café and hold hands as you cross the street to your car.

The clock is ticking and you grow more and more withdrawn. You know that soon you will have to leave him and go and pick up your son. He has already missed his ferry home. You wait in the car while he phones his wife to tell her he'll be late. *I fucking hate this,* he says. *Lying.* You kiss a few times, on the lips but with closed mouths, no tongues. You have to go and get your son. *This was a mistake,* you say. *We shouldn't have met today.* You know this will make it even harder to break off. You are in love with each other. You are both married to other people. It is impossible.

You pick up your son and start the drive home. Inside you, everything feels like it has been pushed up a level. Your stomach is in your chest, your heart is in your throat and your head is spinning. You need to get home. You thunder down country lanes, making small talk with your son, but not listening to anything he says. Too late, you see the lamb. It springs from the bank straight into the bumper. You hit it with a thud. *What was that?* your son says. In the rear-view mirror you see the lamb crumpled at the verge, its legs twisted at odd angles, dead. *I think I hit a pheasant,* you say to your son. *Did you kill the pheasant, Mummy? Is it dead?* he says. *No, darling, I think I just clipped it. I think I saw it run off into the bushes.*

When you get home, your mobile goes off. You move into the living room to answer it, leaving your son eating fish fingers in the kitchen. He is crying hard down the phone to you. *I can't do this,* he sobs. *It's breaking my fucking heart.*

When your husband comes home he finds you crying in the living room. Your son is in the playroom watching a video. Your husband puts his arm around you, pulls you close. *What's up, hon?* he says, *what's the matter? I killed a lamb,* you say. You explain what happened on the drive home. Now you are really crying, as if all the little pains and sadnesses of your life are all coming to the surface at once. *It wasn't your fault,* he says, *the lamb jumped out. You couldn't have avoided it.* You sniff against his chest. *But it was living thing. A beautiful, living thing. And I killed it. I killed it and now it's dead before it even had a chance at life.*

Your husband goes upstairs and runs you a bath. You sit in the hot water, still crying, but less now. He brings you up a mug of hot chocolate. As you bring the hot rim to your lips you can smell the alcohol. *I put some brandy in it,* he says. You hear him putting your son to bed, asking him about his day at school, checking his homework, reading him a story and kissing him goodnight. *I love you, Dad,* you hear your son say. *I love you too,* your husband says as he flicks off the light.

A hundred flowers

Fiona Rintoul

Deng said, *Reform is China's second revolution.* And we believed him. All of us. Even me, the cynical American. 'Now we are moving in the right direction,' I told my husband, Jingyu. 'Now things will change.'

Jingyu was just five years old when his father died in the Hundred Flowers Campaign. *Let a hundred flowers bloom*, Mao said. *Let the hundred schools of thought contend.* People were sceptical. They needed prodding. But in the end they did pour out their criticisms, my father-in-law included. Then the crackdown came.

Still, we were ready to be optimistic about Deng. Almost 30 years had passed since the Hundred Flowers Campaign. And Deng was Deng. I bought a chicken at the market and I roasted it on the fire. I served it with rice and bok choy – an attempt at a Western meal. I used the dollars my family had sent me to buy coffee and chocolate from the Friendship Store, and we had a celebration. Grandma Gao spat the coffee out, but she patted me on the arm as she pottered off on her tiny ruined feet to squat by the door and smoke the Kent cigarettes I'd given her. It was an acceptance of sorts. I looked at my children, their slanting blue eyes and spiky sandy-coloured hair, and I felt a new hope. Perhaps one day I would stop longing for winter when I could swaddle them up against the cries of *lao-wai* that marked them out as foreigners in their own country.

I learned to love Mandarin and Deng Xiaoping at the same time. Our teacher at Swarthmore College used Deng's name to introduce us to tones. It was 1974 and Deng had just been rehabilitated for the first time. Mr Li, a visiting professor from Beijing Normal University who'd stayed on in the US when the Cultural Revolution started, adored Deng. In him he saw hope for his own return to China.

I used to love the shape of Deng's name. Deng is fourth tone, falling sharply; xiao third, diving deep then rising back up; ping second, a steady climb. Together they looked like two hands holding a bowl of warming won-ton soup.

I loved the sounds too: *dung-sheeow-ping.*

'Xiao rhymes with meow,' Mr Li told us, as we struggled with *Pinyin*, the new romanisation system. Mr Li spat on the old Wade-Giles system, which had given the world such woeful mispronunciations as Peking, and which he viewed as function of Western imperialism.

And I loved that Xiaoping meant Little Peace. How much better a name than Bill or Gerry or Fred is Little Peace? And how well it fitted brave little Deng, with his chubby face and his tiny hands, always holding a lit cigarette; little Deng who kept smiling when he was out of favour, who didn't flinch even when the Red Guards pushed his son out a window and made him a paraplegic.

My own name is Camelia Mary Robertson. My mother was a fanciful woman and she pushed my father into second place in the naming game. I was born in Athens, Georgia, my mother's home town, but when I was six years old we moved to Pennsylvania. My father disliked the south. He longed for the north, for industrial Pittsburgh where he'd worked shifts at the steelworks to pay his way through medical school when he first came to the US from Belfast. I grew up in Sewickley Heights, a wealthy borough in Allegheny County, in a large clapboard house painted the colour of pea soup.

My father had high expectations of his children and I'm never entirely sure if I left America to escape his immigrant hopes or to get away from my taut Southern mother. My mother was the kind of woman who wears peach and puts crocheted covers on spare toilet paper rolls.

They didn't approve of my going to Swarthmore – the Kremlin on the Crum, as Spiro T. Agnew once dubbed it. They thought I'd get strange ideas and I did. I marched against the Vietnam War and was carted off by the cops, my hair trailing in the dirt. I joined a Maoist cell of the Communist Party USA. I gave up medicine to study Mandarin Chinese and Eastern Philosophy.

When I announced I was going to China, their disapproval reached a screeching crescendo. My father called me at all hours. 'Your mother can't eat,' he said. Or, 'Your mother's eyes are red raw from crying.' My mother herself called just once. I guessed she'd been down among the dry whites in my father's wine cellar.

'It's shockin',' she said in her Heavens-to-Betsy accent. 'Ma own daughter. Ah don't deserve this. It's–' she paused and snuffled loudly – 'un-American!'

Un-American. It was 1978. Deng had just been named Man of the Year by *Time* magazine. And couldn't she see? Un-American was exactly what I wanted to be.

I believe it's all changed now, but in my day when Americans went to live in China, they travelled one of two routes: either they learned to despise Chinese culture or they learned to despise their own. I took Route 2, but being me, I did it with chutzpah. I wore Mao suits and took Chinese medicine. I practised *Tai chi chuan* and read *The Little Red Book* cover to cover. I excoriated Western critics of China, while excusing sexism and racism within China I'd have gone to the barricades over in my Crum Creek days. When I married Gao Jingyu, a fellow English teacher at the Tianjin Institute of Light Industry, many people were shocked, but I don't believe anyone was surprised.

I've often wondered what would have happened to Jingyu if he hadn't married me. I guess he might have applied to go back north to Harbin instead of bringing his mother and grandmother to Tianjin. And if he had moved to Harbin, had married a slender Chinese woman, lovely as a lotus blossom, he might not have gone to Beijing that day in 1989. If he hadn't had a foreign wife, who in the end would not shut up, could not fit in, Jingyu might not have been in Tiananmen Square when Little Peace sent the tanks in.

By that time, of course, I knew that Little Peace wasn't Deng's real name. His birth name was Xiansheng, an ordinary name. He changed it to Xiaoping in 1924.

I'm back in the US now. Not in Pittsburgh – that would've been too much like coming home. I bought an apartment in San Francisco with the money my father left me.

I feel badly about it. When Jingyu was dying he took my hand and asked me to promise to stay in China, and I promised. Jingyu was a good husband.

My life in China wasn't easy, but he loved me. Not in a honey-I-love-you way, like in the movies. He never said: *I love you*. But he showed it. He showed it in many small ways. I wanted to keep my promise to him. But in the end I couldn't. It didn't work any more. I lived in Tianjin for 25 years and on my last day people stared at me in the street and shouted *lao-wai*.

My children are still in China, grown-up now. My son lives in Hong Kong, using his American passport. My daughter works for an investment firm in Shanghai. When they call me, they sound American, but they're not. My daughter dyes her hair black and wears tinted contact lenses to make her blue eyes look brown. My genes, I sometimes feel, are a rogue element.

Last spring, I visited my daughter in Shanghai. My son came too. The changes were overwhelming, the glitz and the glare. I went into the Peace Hotel to drink tea and I wept. I felt Jingyu and his father had died for nothing. We wanted change. But did we want this?

Later, I tried to talk with my children about their ancestors. I told them they were heroes. They listened for a time, then they said, 'Oh, Mom.' They are proud of them, but they want to move on. And perhaps I don't explain it too well. I've often felt sorry for those two great Chinamen with only an old foreigner to explain their achievements to their descendants.

I guess that's why I decided that when I returned to San Francisco I must do something to honour Jingyu and his father. What I did was this: I ordered a hundred rosebushes from an on-line garden store and I planted them in my allotment. I filled my allotment with rosebushes. When they bloomed, I took a picture of them and I sent it to my children. *Let a hundred flowers bloom*, I wrote on the back. Then, after I'd mailed the picture, I did something I almost never do: I went to Chinatown. There's a café there that serves *Goubuli Baozi*, Tianjin's famous steamed buns. I intended to eat and go, but as I was munching my way through the buns four crumpled old ladies came in to play Mahjong. It was their voices that caught my attention; they spoke the crystal clear Mandarin of educated Beijingese, every tone ringing clean like a bell.

It was beautiful and when I'd finished the buns, instead of signalling for the bill as I'd intended, I asked the waitress to bring me some green tea. After all, I thought, why rush home? Why not sit a while and listen?

Static

Deborah Andrews

For weeks after, I found myself counting back the hours to figure out what time it was in Los Angeles, where Suzanne lived. Usually at the end of the day, when I helped mother into bed, or during lunchtimes as I stared out of the office window turning a bite of cheese sandwich slowly round in my mouth. Sometimes, if I woke in the middle of the night, I would think of Suzanne finishing at the studio and wonder what she'd have planned for the evening. I looked again and again at the photos she had emailed, zooming in on her mouth, nose and brown eyes. And of course, when I felt sure that mother was asleep, I listened to the cassette. Over and over. My ear next to the speaker, straining for anything I might have missed.

So, Suzanne, you've come here to see me today because you have some unresolved issues in your life, am I right?

I don't know, really... A friend of mine came to see you last year, and she said that you really helped her move on with some stuff.

Well, first of all, Suzanne, I can sense you've had a really difficult year.

It's been a tough year, yeah...

Okay, honey. I want you to know right now that there are a lot of people here in this room with us today who really care about you. Okay?

Okay...

So, I hear the reservation in your voice, and I want you to relax. Any funny business – furniture flying about the place, exploding light bulbs – that's just stupid B-movie film stuff, okay? Okay. I want you to tell me if the name Christine or Claire means anything to you?

My mom's name was Celia...

Yes. Celia. That's right. Well, she's here with us, Suzanne. She's a very beautiful lady. She's smiling and she wants you to know that she's at peace now. She's standing here with an older lady and a man in a brown suit. And they all love you very much... Okay?

Okay...

The name Elena... Does that mean anything to you...?

No... I don't think so...

Never mind... Oh! You lost someone recently. Just before Easter...?

Yes. My dad.

Do you ever just kind of know something? Like you'll have a tune going round and round in your head, and when you turn on the radio it's playing? That's how it was when I first saw Suzanne. We'd arranged to meet in Sorrento's, but as I walked across the railway bridge I looked down and felt as if someone had flicked a switch in my chest. I thought, That's her. But I didn't run to catch her up. I wanted to see how she moved, what she did when she got to the zebra crossing, what things caught her eye. She was a little taller than I thought she would be, and wore a yellow skirt that finished just above the knee, showing her tanned legs. She'd tied her blonde hair up. Although she had said in an email that she was thirty-six, in many ways she still looked like a girl. I wished I'd at least thought to put a colour rinse through my greying mop. I lingered for a couple of minutes outside the camera shop opposite Sorrento's, feigning an interest in telescopic lenses whilst summoning up some courage. Then I propelled myself forward, doubting I was ready, my stomach pedalling backwards.

'Suzanne?' I said. 'I'm Edith.'

Yes, that was your most recent loss. Your father. Matthew?

Michael.

That was very sad, Suzanne. But Michael wants you to know that he became unconscious at the time of the collision, and the rest was just like slowly falling into a dream. He knows that you loved him very much, even if sometimes you did fight like cat and dog...

Okay...

He's saying he wants you to use that money he left you. Does that make sense?

Yes.

He wants you to move on with your life, and have some fun again... I'm still getting the name Evie or Ellie, no?

I don't think so...

After we had drunk a cup of coffee and discussed her journey, our home towns and vocations, I suggested that we take a walk down by the river. We sat on the grass; I knew that I'd find it a bit uncomfortable, but I thought it would be less formal than a bench. Suzanne slipped her shoes off and her feet were longer and slimmer than mine. I looked at where my hand lay in the grass, my fleshy knuckles, the distance between my fingers and her leg. Her skin was tighter, smoother, eighteen years younger. And I had a strange desire to... I don't know. Touch her leg, maybe. After a while she put her sunglasses on, let her hair loose from its ponytail and lay back. I undid my buckles, took off my sandals and lined them up next to her strappy gold shoes.

'A butterfly,' she said, pointing upwards and smiling.

I caught a glimpse of it just as it fluttered out of sight.

'A Cabbage White,' I said, feeling a sense of pride, as if I was somehow personally responsible for the fine summer's day and all the pleasing things in it. I didn't repeat mother's usual complaint that Cabbage Whites wreck gardens.

Now, your father was married twice. Right, Suzanne?

Yes.

And firstly he was married in England. Wait...he was an Englishman?

That's right.

Do you know much about your father's family?

He still has a brother in England, but I don't think they ever really got on...

And your father's first wife, Jean...?

Joan, I think.

Yes. She's not a well lady now...

Actually, she died a long time ago.

Really? Suzanne, I'm not getting that...

Yes, she died before dad met my mom.

I'm sorry to say this to you, Suzanne, but Michael is telling me it's the right

*thing to do. That he wants you to know. Joan is still alive and lives in the south
of England with...that's her name – Edith.*

As the afternoon wore on we drifted into a comfortable silence, so it came as
quite a surprise when Suzanne said, 'So, what did you know about *our father?*'
It was odd, how she said Our Father. The first thing I thought of was the Lord's
Prayer. Her question was too direct, I thought. But that's the Americans for
you.

'My mother didn't really speak about Michael,' I said, the words
Philandering Bastard echoing in my head. It was the only time I had heard
mother swear. I didn't ask her about him again after that.

'Well,' Suzanne said, 'he was a really kind and generous man. He had a
great sense of humour. He was good at organising family days out, picnics
and amusement parks, that sort of thing. He loved the outdoors and built
me a tree house in the garden. He taught me to drive as soon as I was old
enough.'

'That sounds... lovely,' I said.

Suzanne sat up and took her sunglasses off.

'You've got his eyes,' she said. 'Just exactly the same colour of blue.'

I looked at the cormorant standing on a bare branch of a dead tree half
sunk in the middle of the river. On the bank a little boy was throwing bread
to the swans and Canadian geese. Looking at my own feet I realised that the
walk had rubbed a nasty blister on the heel of my right foot. It nipped as I put
my sandals back on.

Who's Edith?

*He's asking you to forgive him, Suzanne. And he's asking, as a last request,
that you contact Edith. That you tell Joan and Edith that he is truly very sorry.
He wants his daughter, Edith, to know that he loved her, that he never stopped
caring about her.*

Suzanne emailed three more times after she got back to Los Angeles. I let her
last email sit in my inbox for two months. And then, on my birthday, I looked
once more at all the photos and correspondence she had sent and deleted

the whole lot. Mother's back was really bad by then, but I helped her into her wheelchair and put a blanket across her knee. Her eyes were watery, but still blue. Blue, just like mine. I pushed her down to the river, stopping once by the post office to drop the cassette – broken and wrapped in several carrier bags – into the litter bin.

'What's wrong?' mother said.

'Nothing.'

'Why did we stop?'

'I had something stuck to the bottom of my shoe.'

It was late autumn and, along the grassy verge, the wheels of mother's chair gathered damp, brown leaves.

'Where are we going?' she asked. 'And why are you not at work?'

'It's my birthday,' I said. 'And we're going to Sorrento's for a bite of lunch.'

'Extravagant,' she said.

'Yes,' I said, 'and you can have anything you like for under six pounds. But I knew she'd only want a slice of ham and an egg.'

'It's us girls,' she said, 'isn't it? Us girls, together.'

The anniversary

Elinor Brown

Two bodies undulating on a sea wave, pillowed on each other's mouths, hands smoothing human silk in perfect union. It's like that for the exhibitionist lovers on the billboard across the street, but not for us. You're late, you barely bother to greet me when you come in. Romance lies skewered in the basement, it seems courtesy was next in line. Dinner was ready an hour ago; you sit down at the table ready to be waited on and watch me dishing it up, I should throw it at you.

The plates chink and squeak as we eat. Sitting opposite me, you hunch over your bowl, as if casting your shadow over it will make a little eating room of your own – a hutch. That's what you do, you hutch. I want to be your food, included in that space of yours, enshrined in your shadow. I want you to devour me, the way you tear meat off a bone. Instead I talk and you don't listen, don't even pretend to, and my food tastes of nothing. Sometimes it gets so sterile in here, you could be wearing a surgeon's robes, carrying a dish of bloody implements to the sink for me to wash.

The water is warm and my fingers tingle as I search for shipwrecked cutlery. You mould in behind me and stroke the strands of hair from my neck, while your other hand, fizzing with a scoop of bubbles glides up the inside of my thigh. You would have done that once, but now you slope out of the kitchen to commune with the TV. I watched it last and I feel you wince as you lower the volume. It makes me squirm. I shrink into the sofa and doze to the sound of water cascading through old pipes.

'I've run you a bath,' your voice and the water call me back.

I don't want a bath, I want to talk and I want you to hear me. I want you to keep your promises, remember the ones we made to each other before God and all those carefully chosen witnesses? They were meant to last the whole of our earthly life together, that illuminated day when a lifetime did not seem enough.

Why don't you join me? I should ask you and break down this wall, it might even be that simple, but doubt chokes me. I peel myself from the sofa, crumpling newsprint; the paper wafts to the floor and settles with its tip lapping at my coffee. I'm staring at you, watching me, and I can't remember the last time I really looked at you. You have silver skeins through your hair and loose skin around your eyes and yet you look so lost within your indelible age, you could be a child. This moment of seeing unbalances me. I have spent so much time trying to make you suffer.

'Do you still love me?' my words spatter out like accidental gunfire.

'Sorry?'

'Nothing. I said, thanks.'

Emotion darts across your face. Remorse?

I lie defenceless in the bath, embalmed in watery arms scented with lavender. Weals of heat flower on my legs. I shrivel slowly. There's a patch on the bathroom ceiling, growing like a cancerous mole. The water cools and I push myself out, my stomach is a taut clothesline, the rest of my body drips off. In a parallel universe, I emerge from a temple of steam, crowned with a fluffy white turban, bare shoulders bejewelled with water beads bursting down to the small of my back. Back in the real world the towel rasps against my skin, which is still damp as I put on my old, holey T-shirt, a token of a package holiday romance, when love was a seashore kiss, intoxicated with the salty breathes and rushes of evening breeze on sun-saturated skin. I can't believe I still have it, perhaps I should have accepted his invitation to France. I could have been Madame Chopard of Rouen.

Our toothbrushes sit thrust together by habit in the crusty mire at the depths of a chipped glass. I take yours, frayed at the edges from rigorous activity. My tongue searches for a time when adoration for everything you touched made me tremble. The toothpaste catches the back of my throat and burns. Will you be repulsed by the cold soggy sensation of a recently used brush in your mouth? Do you look at mine in disgust, like someone else's dirty fridge? I can't tell any more.

It's been a hellish day and it ain't over yet. I brace myself when I put my key in the lock. It opens after one turn – she's home. I don't know why I thought she wouldn't be, the triumph of hope over experience. On summer nights she used to sit and wait for me on the steps outside and smother me with kisses before dragging me inside to show me her latest addition to the flat or feed me some new dish she'd invented. Once I came home to find the whole place flickering in the soft, quiet light of a hundred candles. She lay naked on the kitchen table, my supper spread across her body. I can see her so vividly it could have been yesterday, but it must have been our first year here, a different lifetime.

The flat is tranquil when I fill it with my silence. But it's only a moment before I can hear her waiting for me to say hello. Haven't we been together long enough for her make the first move? Her mood is visible, it precedes her, lime green and mercurial. As I walk into the kitchen I'm surprised for a moment by how attractive she is. She's made chicken soup again, for my soul or hers? The smell, sickly sweet, makes my mouth water.

She's talking at me. I've donned my protective deafness and the sounds make no sense. How do you love someone who makes you feel like you're biting on tin foil? Her chair scrapes across the floor, more scratches, I must put some felt under the feet. I'm still hungry but she's chucked her food in the bin and is taking out her aggression on the washing up. I should say something conciliatory, touch her as I put my plate beside the sink, but she's surrounded herself with a force field of anger and I have no idea how to break through. It's almost as if she revels in it, this dark, frigid atmosphering. She'd be far better off living in some old Russian novel.

I edge out of the kitchen and turn on the TV and the brass section of the ten o'clock news blasts through me. Why does she always turn up the volume? The news is depressing in a dull, predictable way. More flood and famine, and streams of sick, starving people. The elections are a sleaze-fest, mistresses galore, but I'm starting to think, 'Can you blame them?' We've got years stretching ahead of us and it already feels like an eternity. What was it the vicar said? Something about marriage 'bringing us together in the delight and tenderness of sexual union and joyful commitment to the end of our lives'. A juicy lie followed by a contradiction. He should have gone into politics.

I've seen enough so I go and run her bath and light the candles round the edge, an old habit. There's safety in ritual. I'm not as jaded as I think, the ravaged faces of the flood victims on the news follow me to the bathroom. We have so much and it is never enough. Would we love each other more if life were tougher, sparser, if we lived in the real world? A disaster would strip us down to the essentials.

She's half asleep, curled on the kitchen sofa with the papers in the crook of her arm like a comfort rag. Her face is peaceful, beautiful. I don't know if I can approach her yet, so I keep my distance and tell her I've run her bath. She opens her eyes and stares at me.

She tries to rise, still sleepy, and mumbles something. Before I register it – and I am too late to stop myself asking her what she said – the moment is gone and she's slamming the bathroom door, wishing it were my head. I wish it were too. I'm sure she just asked me if I still love her.

A story without a place

J L Williams

I

What took so long to make now gone, more present in its absence than it ever was, defined by who it once touched, where it once lay, how it once saw. Fragile silkworm's cocoon of memory, not fractured much as drifting wafts of cloud or smoke between which stars or sky are sometimes visible... reminding that the universe is filled with so much space where it could be somewhere, somehow not troubling anyone any more, weightless as breath or shadow.

He is so far away there is nothing around he even knows a name for. Days pass. The sinking of birds, the words of his only book.

I am a secret man, he says to himself.

He sleeps, he wraps himself in a white sheet. There are some dreams, not many. Often the face of the girl, sometimes another face, he wakes confused. He drinks black coffee. He weeps.

There are the colours of her, the dried leaf black of her hair, the salmon pink flesh of her mouth. Her teeth like the whites of eyes, her, he cannot do this for long. What was that poem, 'her eyes are nothing...'

Walking, running sometimes. Sitting. Eating, because he has to. Drinking, because he has to. Not a smoker.

The space between ends of words, between minds, between lips from which words come out, she said, what was it she said?

Where was he when she, when he...

Black wings, black hair over a white face. Sujuki, Tamora.

Rain. Red sun. A cherry burst with a pin. Not just commitment, a vow.

What is a vow? He remembers wondering to himself. Sheets of silver, impenetrable longing. The sort of mist one breathes in.

Where was she when he?

Her mouth, so many holes in her for entering and exiting. The violable paths of love, her leaves, her roots, the trellis she climbed to wake, the sun at her throat.

He reads these lines from his book aloud,

'Whose trespass in the carnal void

Will echo footsteps to the heart,'

on his knees, as if in prayer, weeping. From some radio Maria Callas's low tremolo guts him, he is sick.

One woman, another woman, a child. He realises that the old story is new when it happens to you, he falls down.

His eyes are stars. He is concave. Stick figures gesture. Between the dreams of their faces – light, the passing of air through his body. Tamora, Sujuki. A foetus without a name, never to have a name, this child, his child, their child, her. She.

I wonder what her laughter would have sounded like, he says.

A dog with white teeth bites his leg. It thinks his leg is a stick. He does not scream. He understands the terms and conditions of his punishment, that after the frenzy the dogs will be tired and thirsty. He pulls the white sheet around him. Dreams.

A girl with blossoms in her hair. When she breathes out she exhales a mist that wraps him in pain. His only choice is to breathe in, but he is afraid. He knows that this is how she will enter him.

He wakes.

I am a lonely man, he says to himself.

Sun, white burning reflection off glass. Beethoven bears down on him out of the dark mouth of some radio. He screams. Thinks about fish, about the biggest fish that refused to be caught, even in death a thing beyond things. He thinks of his wife, of his lover, of his daughter – all dead.

His fingers are sticks of a cherry tree. His breath is blossoms. Black wings of hair fold over his face.

I have broken the law of myself, he says.

II

Though you never knew me and will never know me you recognise me in strangers and blank stares. You think it is your self you see. You wonder how you could have lost me so early on but my eyes are your eyes. My voice is your voice. My loneliness is yours.

Here, here is what happened.

He married a young girl, took a vow to love her above all others. He said yes to this vow though he did not know what it meant or, to put it properly, he did not understand the implications. The girl shook as she placed the ring on his finger.

Two years later the girl was pregnant and he became scared. He shaved. He changed the way he dressed. He was seen less and less.

The girl grew fat with child and fell asleep most nights alone.

One morning he came in to find them dead.

An anonymous letter lay on the floor detailing the affair he was having with another woman.

His wife had cut open her wrists.

He was so devastated that he, in anger, broke off his affair with his lover.

After repeated and increasingly desperate attempts to change his mind, his lover shot herself in the heart and died instantly.

Doctors and the press said it was a near impossible shot, but she managed.

He ran, lost himself in sickness mixed with insanity, lost himself almost completely, but could not quite let go.

He believed in the imagination, in the individual's right to come to their own conclusion.

And so, in spite of himself, he survived the mauling of dogs, the itinerant meandering, the days of starvation and the nights of sickness.

His wounds healed and he became a man again, with a look in his eyes that warned strangers away, that frightened children.

He ate rice and seaweed.

He walked most nights, unable or unwilling to sleep.

He never let himself love until he came across a woman who seemed familiar to him.

She sat with a nonchalance that he recognised, the feigned indifference of one who has suffered great pain.

They did not speak, but he watched her for some time, comforted by the fact that it seemed death had come for her too and that she had refused, for the time being, his offer.

As he watched her walk away a concern wrenched at his heart – that it was a mistake not to speak to her, that all his life had in some way led him to this potential meeting.

Then he remembered how many more words would be required for that story, that his second vow was the one he could never break, and knowing what sort of effect his love had on women he knew he could not speak to her, or any other woman, ever again. Not in an egotistical way. In a totally honest way.

When she left the question he asked himself, he who had destroyed everything that could ever be a home, was, 'How can anyone love a man who has no place?'

A valid excuse for avoiding all but one, she who knows everything and nothing, a girl who never had a place at all.

Who was it he saw? Who am I?

A ghost. But I would have been about her age. My hair would have been that long and black, my tongue that pink, my lips that red, my skin that white.

Here, here her features fade away.

III

Time, whose life depends on ours, keeps its secrets as only the best lovers can – those we meet in passing, in places with no name, where joys exist purely and are possessed completely though not at all.

An apple sat on the glass-topped chest of drawers.

Clothes lay scattered.

He still filled the air; his scent, the ripple of each word he had spoken.

I don't believe in love, he'd said again and again.

She could feel in her fingertips the softness of the wool of his vest. She could feel where he had been inside her, how he had made her skin fall from her body in waves.

She wondered if his wife had traced the marks in his back she had made, if she knew her smell on his fingers, his belly, the arches of his feet, his lips.

What had come to her while he was holding her was the image of a horse jumping high waves. Each wave that came was higher than the last and each time the horse strained that much more to clear the wave. It raised its head and tightened the muscles in its flanks. Froth dripped from its fetlocks and long tail. How much higher could the horse jump? Could it keep jumping higher and higher forever?

She ate the apple slowly, savouring each crisp mouthful. Juice ran out the side of her mouth and she licked it feeling how his tongue had traced the shape of her lips.

How cold it was.

She looked at his face in her mind's eye. It seemed as if she could never be alone as long as she could remember, this.

All around her blossoms fell like snow. She raised the gun to her breast.

I believe in love, she said again and again.

Death and other distractions

Liam Murray Bell

This is how Joe died. Just over a year ago, when I was sixteen, Joe Kavanagh fell five storeys from a tenement window and landed on the concrete pavement below. He broke his neck, cheekbone, collarbone, arm and wrist. Two vertebrae in his back were fractured. The ambulance that took him to the Western Infirmary did so only in order to have him pronounced dead. Everything else the paramedics and doctors did was routine. He had died on impact. Joe Kavanagh was my best friend.

We had been to a gig that night. A friend of a friend played bass guitar for the band. They were called Death Rattle. Heavy metal. They were local celebrities for a while around the West End of Glasgow. Anyway, me and Joe had managed a bottle of wine each before the gig, six pints of watered-down beer during, and then he had half a bottle of brandy afterwards. He was drinking brandy because it was the only thing in the liquor cabinet at Hayley's flat. Hayley was Joe's girlfriend. She was an attractive girl. They had been going out for three months. Young love and all that.

So, we were up at Hayley's flat after the gig (her parents' flat really) and Joe was by the window smoking. He was by the window because Hayley's house had a strict no-smoking policy. The window was open. He turned to talk to us all with a drunken grin on his face and leant backwards against it. One moment he was there, the next he was gone. He fell five storeys. This is how Joe died.

Like I say, this happened over a year ago. Things have moved on since then. Certainly, they have. At first, things were difficult. The funeral was all flowers and weeping teachers. Then there was collective grief counselling at school for anyone who had known Joe, no matter how remotely. Hayley didn't go to our school. Even at home, my mother sat me down and we had a talk about Heaven. It was worse than the birds and the bees conversation. No one seemed to understand. All I wanted was to just get away from it all. To be numb.

Which is why I threw myself at the books. What I mean is, I began to study hard. I began to think about university. There were no more parties or gigs. I finished school with five A-grade Highers. This isn't my way of bragging, by the way, it's actually relevant. You see, with five Highers, I had no need to attend a sixth year at school. Instead, I was accepted onto the English Literature course at Glasgow University. I began lectures three months ago.

All this, you might say, has nothing to do with Joe. It does, though. You see, he was a keen writer. He used to sit in his room and write these comic pieces that read like something Douglas Adams would have written. You know the kind of thing I mean, quirky and offbeat humour with a bit of science fiction thrown in. We even had a go at writing some lyrics for Death Rattle together. The band didn't like them. Too poetic, they said. Anyway, I wasn't just going to university for myself, I was doing it for Joe as well.

Maybe Hayley had the same idea. Probably not. I don't really know why she ended up choosing the same course as I did, but there she was on my first day of term. There she was. I hadn't seen her since Joe's funeral. Not only did she go to a different school, she also hung around with a different crowd. The Death Rattle crowd.

She was looking good. When Joe and she had gone out, she had worn band hoodies and ripped jeans, her nails had been bitten short and she had a habit of chewing on the loose strands of her blond hair. You could still see she was pretty, though. She had this snub nose, as though someone had squashed it with the tip of their finger. It's hard to describe. Not only that, she also had these rippling dimples that creased her cheeks every time she smiled. When I saw her at that first lecture, she still had all these things, but more. She was no longer nervous and she no longer chewed her hair. She wore a cut-off denim skirt. When she smiled, not only did her cheeks crease, her whole face became animated.

'Hi,' she said. 'Long time, no see.'

'Aye,' I replied.

'In fact, I've not seen you since– ' She paused. 'How are you?'

I shrugged. 'Could be worse.' Suddenly, I wanted to get away, to lose myself amongst the milling crowd of students. 'You?' I asked, cursing my own politeness.

'Pretty good, thanks. Mind if I sit with you?'

'Not at all,' I said.

After that, we began sitting beside each other every day. We compared notes. I even began to bring packets of sweets for us to share. It started off innocently: a packet of mints, a bar of chocolate, but it quickly escalated to miniature Toblerone, and packets of Rolos. I even let her have the last one. I hated myself for it. Every time she turned to me and smiled sweetly, I was confronted not only by the stab of desire in my chest, but also by the image of Joe. Joe grinning as he fell backwards.

Which brings me to the present. Or rather, not quite the present. Yesterday, actually. I had been wanting to ask Hayley out for the last few weeks, you see. That is, part of me wanted to ask her out and part of me was so repelled by the idea that I stayed away from lectures for a full week. Flu, I told her. It was going around. It didn't matter in the end, anyway. She was the one that asked me.

'What're you doing after this?' she asked. We were in a lecture about Alexander Pope. It wasn't very interesting. I had been trying not to squint at the gap between the top two buttons of her shirt. Trying not to catch a glimpse of her black bra with the laced pink pattern.

'Nothing much. Why?' I flushed and looked up into her eyes.

'I thought we could go to the park, maybe, and catch up?'

'Sounds good to me.'

Hayley had packed a picnic. Sandwiches, crisps, and a half dozen bottles of cloudy cider. It was a bright day with a sharp bite of frost in the air. Only two weeks until Christmas. Even so, the sun was high in the sky. We sat on the banks of the River Kelvin and watched the torrent of muddy water. Huddled in jackets and scarves, we drank from the bottles of cider. She was onto her second by the time I was halfway down my first. The sandwiches and crisps went largely untouched.

'You blame me,' she said, after her third bottle. 'Don't you?' She looked down at the fast-running water and twisted the cap from a fresh bottle.

'For what?'

'Joe.'

I was silent.

'Do you?'

'Of course I don't.'

She looked doubtful. I couldn't find the words to reassure her, so instead I just smiled. It felt tight and unnatural on my face, frozen in place by the chill air. She shivered. I placed an arm around her shoulder and drew her towards me.

'Do you still think about him?' she asked.

'Of course I do.'

'And?'

'And what?'

'What do you think of?'

I shrugged. 'I don't know. What do you think of?'

'I don't know. Just him.'

She laid her head against my shoulder. It felt natural. Like folding my arms, or crossing my legs. An extension of my body. The world had become fluid around me, the jagged edges of the trees and the cold of the air curbed by the soft haze of the cider. I felt wonderful. And confused.

Her silken blond hair tickled the skin of my cheek, drawing my face down to rest against the top of her head. Yet she knew things about Joe that I would never know. The setting was perfect, the winter sun blistering the cloudless sky. Then again, she had shared times like these with Joe. She had placed her head upon his shoulder. Getting to know her again had been like rediscovering a forgotten part of myself. Yet she had been with Joe. I looked forward to seeing her every day. But what about Joe? Her body was nestled so comfortably against mine. But Joe.

I decided to kiss her.

Leaning over, I kissed her on the forehead.

She mumbled something.

'What was that?' I asked softly, stroking her cheek.

No answer.

I leant down further until my lips were just inches away from her own.

She was snoring softly with a peaceful smile etched upon her face.

A Christmas miracle

E G J

My brother's wife and I go way back. In fact, I was the one who brought them
together. I am reminded of this as I watch Maryam enter through the glass
and brass door of the café, a Christmas decoration to her left, a flashing Santa,
making her face shift, red white, red white. She does a little twirl, takes in the
room, our eyes snatch on each other's, sudden static, white noise in my ears.
A small, gloved hand comes up to wave at me, points to the counter, smile,
nod. She winks and blows me a kiss. Her blue cape moves in fluid motion, as
if of its own accord. She turns around and her back is to me, she is leaning
across the counter (I imagine the round fullness of her pink breasts under
that white shirt pressing against the marble, everything is breast height to
her, she is abreast with the situation, pint-sized, my brother's wife), ordering
hot chocolate with extra whipped cream from the baffled boy behind it. Of
course, most people look slightly baffled at a distance. I meet my own eyes in
the mirror wall behind him. Look away.

Maryam and I met in the university library. I was working extra there, trying
to make ends meet. I had decided to go for my own flat, never was much of
the sharing type. You grow up with an older sibling, it's all you get: share
this, share that, hand-me-down trousers, toys, dreams. At nineteen, I wanted
something of my own, an uninvaded space, a place to just be me. Still, there
on my topmost shelf: Kenny's battered teddy, Kenny's collection of illicit bottle caps. Stolen treasure, that I treasured the more for it. To work I wore his
faded Nirvana T-shirt under my own purple waistcoat. Maryam was there
every night, slaving away on her term paper. She did sociology, something
like that. Social work. She was always carrying heavy books around from

there to here and back again. It looked like an exercise program, a surreal
version of a Victorian work-out: to improve a young lady's posture, balancing
acts with the Holy Bible, heavy stuff. After a couple of days of watching from
the aisles, I offered to carry some of the books for her, I couldn't help myself,
she was so small. Myself, I have always been willowy, long arms just made
for carrying books, bad joke, awkward shuffle. 'Oh, thank you!' she said, and
after closing time she took me out for drinks. I had half expected her to be
drinking girly stuff, peach schnapps, white wine spritzers, but she liked her
single malts doubled, neat. I had a Guinness, two, three, straight to my head,
I was scrawny in those days, and hadn't had a bite since lunch. When the pub
closed she made some joke about her room mate's noise levels, innocent wide
eyes, as if we didn't both know she'd be coming home with me.

'Hey there, stranger.'
      Her cheeks are flushed with the sudden warmth of the hot beverage. Her
lips glisten like she just licked them, pink tongue, stray cream.
      'So,' she says, exhales, as she falls into the armchair I have kept for her. 'I
haven't seen you for ages. How's Glasgow treating you these days?'
      'Och, you know. Same as always. It's been too long though, Maryam, it
really has.'
      'I know!' She uses the 'O' of her mouth to blow on the mug she has raised
in front of her. 'I've missed you! I miss us,' she says, oblivious, lips quivering
slightly in anticipation of the first sip. 'Remember how we used to be?'

I remember how we used to be. You'd have thought I'd be over it by now, some
kind of instinct for self-preservation erasing it all, the way you get with old relationships; years later you have no idea what you used to do with that person,
what you saw in each other. You just don't remember, you forget without even
making the conscious decision to do so. It's called moving on, I know. The mem-
ories are fuzzy, though, I'll say that, dreamlike: Maryam in my bed, me in the red
wing chair, and then, and then mingled up, she moves in her sleep, the duvet,
my hands. Her eyes open and God and God it is everything, I think her eyes are
going to flow over and then they do. How many nights? This game. How many
weeks, months? Not quite half a year and not a word. I should have spoken, I
know. It was unfair, it's always unfair to expect the other to speak first.

'I miss you too.'

'Kenny and I are so happy,' she says, confusedly.

We stare at each other for a bit, neither of us quite sure what she means by that.

'I mean,' she says, falls silent. Her fingers fiddle with the elongated tea spoon, staining the snowy napkin cocoa brown. Hidden speakers play Last Christmas. I want to do unspeakable things to George Michael's vocal chords.

'What's up, Maryam?'

She looks up at me then, straight into me, and she smiles that smile, the dream-time smile, the Maryam-in-love smile that I haven't seen for so long, I was beginning to think I'd imagined it, that I'd imagined it all along, that she had so consummately wished we'd never happened she had somehow managed to erase it from objective history, if there is such a thing. Things that happen behind closed doors are only tenuously real, anyway. There's no real link, no real link unless you leave some physical manifestation, unless there is a witness, unless you choose to make it known.

'I'm pregnant,' she says, her hands shaking. The mug clatters against the side plate, the spoon, an infinitesimal tremor moving through the wood of the table and up my arms, into me, as she always gets into me, too easy, pitiful, into me. 'I wanted you to be the first to know.'

I have heard this before. Seven years ago, in the serving area of the Queen Margaret Union. Maryam clutching at my hands, my foolish, foolish hands, imagining themselves quite loved, held, till death, all that. She leans into me and I blush, thinking that everyone will see, everyone will finally see.

'I am in love with your brother. I wanted you to be the first to know. I think he wants me too.'

'I want you.'

Blank silence. She stares into space, her coffee cooling, untouched, on the table. Her index finger is stroking my left thumb.

'It'll be great, you know. I want children. You know that. I've always wanted children. It's what I'm meant to do.'

'Does Kenny know?'

'Not yet,' Maryam leans her head on my shoulder, playfully, for all the world to see and not to see. She looks up at me, soft eyes, soft face, soft lips. 'I'll tell him tonight.'

'I'm so excited!' She scrunches up the cocoa-stained napkin. Her mug is already half-empty, the milk skins clinging to the sides, the algae in a murky aquarium. 'I thought it would never happen. You know how long I have wanted to have his child. Now we'll be a real family, for real. And you will have a nephew. My child's aunt will be my best friend!'

'Aha.'

'I only just found out,' she's glancing at her own reflection in the window, combing a stray wisp of hair back behind her ear. It has grown quite dark outside, already. The street lights tick on, one by one. Straining my eyes, I see a woman pass by, a child on her hip, her face white, orange, blue. She looks stressed, uncomfortable. It's in the way she walks. Something not quite right. The wean's hands go up to her throat, as if to throttle her. Pat, stroke, pinch. They cross to the other side of the street.

'I'm going to tell Kenny tonight. Didn't want to do it over the phone, can you imagine it? He'd get nothing done all day. Besides– ' Maryam leans in. For a second, I want to lean across and kiss her. Would she notice? Would anyone? Just one swift graze of my lips against hers, the barest caress, before it all ends. 'I was meeting you today. I wanted you to know before everyone. Like it used to be. That's what I want. We love you so much, honey. You really should come and visit more often. I get so lonely here without you.'

'Aha. Look, Maryam, I don't know how to tell you this...'

Her face is all lit-up innocence. Already the blooming virgin, haloed by multi-coloured fairy lights.

'Kenny's sterile,' I say.

Nothing more to say.

'The devout observer, devoted' – a short story by Gabriel MacNicol

C J Begg

Say, my friend, now *this* is a parable. At our modern building in summer, ground floor, towards the rear. The corridor to the refreshment machine: short, hot and dark beneath my black-eyed lens. A light flickers under many-score wings of moths, but still I see all.

Now the woman – poor woman – she stood with her back to him, unawares, while the man – idiotic and lustful boy – stared at her back, or more specifically the upper third of it. A hank of henna-tinted hair drooped from under the grey satin of her hijab, pulled out by the cable of her telephone headset. As she bent to strike the machine, the lock of hair snaked forward, curling at the root of her left breast. She stood and adjusted her strumpet attire, cursing at her thwarted purchase. The depraved *shaz* approached her.

'Playing up again?' he said.

'Aye, took my money. The can's stuck but. So thirsty.'

Sluttishly, she rolled her eyes and looked at him – the grinning, lecherous cunt-struck infidel.

'Let me try,' he said.

With his limp wrist he placed a coin in the slot and pressed. If only she knew of his degeneracy. Nothing happened. He laughed and pressed again. Smiling like a harlot, she leaned into his breath.

'It's nice to be alone with you,' she said. 'I'm glad we met up like this.'

'You are? It's okay. I mean everything's okay, aye?'

'I had a good time. Didn't you have a good time?'

'Of course,' he whispered. 'Do we really have to... '

The filthy sodomite was embarrassed – he could not in words relive that which so reviles even himself. He stood back from her and shifted his weight to one foot then the other, balancing his conscience.

'I'm sorry, I didn't mean that. You're a good friend,' he said.

'Oh. A friend?'

She examined her impure hands. He took them, but she pulled away.

'What else can we be? Let's be realistic, eh?'

'We could see each other again,' she said.

'I don't have a death wish.'

For that, the proud sister slapped him across his sallow cheek. He held his jawbone and laughed.

'Good illustration. As I said, I'm only being realistic.'

'You're being realistic? You've been flirting with me for two years. Was that realistic?'

'But look at what... at who you are,' he said.

'Excuse me?'

He paused, as if there was some point to choosing what foul words came next from his idiot mouth.

'I don't agree with your culture.'

'You mean my religion,' she said.

'I have no time for any religion, but more especially it's this.'

His Kafir fingers taunted the sweet cloth of her hijab.

'I mean why? Oppression? Empowerment? Not modesty anyway...'

Her hand was raised again in warning, then paused as if to caress. Only the intent was still wrathful.

'I cannae not wear it,' she said. 'You should know that.'

'Your family again?'

'Aye. My big brothers. They're all a bit Allah-happy.'

'Seemed nice to me,' he said.

'You think that now. You don't understand everything.'

'So at ten years old they had you engaged to some goat-fucker, aye?'

'No. Don't be offensive. We can't all be born into Daddy's oil money.'

'I got this job on my own merit.'

'Of course.'

'We weren't talking about me. What do I not understand?'

'Nothing,' she said.

Now *his* hands were raised, like a shrugging Jew. He could not conceal his true lineage: he may've been bred in this cold land, but the blood of Solomon was in the boy for sure.

'So? They want you to move back home, leave your auntie's place?'

'I'll tell you if we see more of each other.'

'I saw plenty...'

He winked. And with that wink she was re-cast: the smiling flirt, returning the unbeliever's joke, his immoral innuendo. Again he moved towards her holy covering.

'Anybody can see you're a bad Muslim. But you're so...'

She laughed, a dirty little laugh, then startled. A cleaning woman passed, her trolley rattling, upended mop heads dancing. She turned her head from the two fornicators and muttered. But the whore continued, whispering:

'There's still much more to see.'

'But there's so much to lose, think of what might happen to you.'

'You mean to *you*.'

'Never mind about me,' he said.

'My brothers would cut your bollocks off.'

'They'd have to find us. We could run away – I am a master of disguise – and would anyone recognise you without that thing?

Her laugh again, a degenerate rattle.

'Probably not, but I couldn't,' she said.

'Come on. Why not?'

'You've changed your tune,' she said.

'Eh?'

'Very keen all of a sudden.'

'I like you. You, you know I like you,' he said.

'You like me... well at least you've made up your mind on something.'

She held his hand and pushed him back into the void, the hussy's booth between the refreshment machine and the window. There the Jezebel kissed him long and soft on the lips. The hungry fool returned the kiss then broke away. An apostate before Baal, he then sank to his knees and took her hand to his mouth.

'I can't,' he said.

'I'm going to punch you this time. I really am. You're realistic, you fancy me, you want to run away together, you "like" me. What's the problem? We had a nice time, we could have more of the same.'

'Aye,' he said.

'Are you three or 23?' she asked.

'You don't know everything about me.'

'So you're married with five weans? Is that it?'

'It just wouldn't work,' he insisted.

'It's simple as I see it,' she replied.

He smiled a fake smile.

'I love it when you smile at me,' she said.

'It wouldn't work, trust me. Aye, on one level it is dead simple. I mean I really fancy you, but I don't think you understand wh.... I don't want to hurt you, but I'm so mixed up.'

'I know what I'd be getting into. I'm not crazy,' she said.

'You don't know what you're getting at all. Christ.'

The blasphemer sank back against the wall. He struck the machine hard with his puny fist. Nothing moved, except the bitter tear that sprung in his debauched grey eyes.

'Fucking machine. Still thirsty?' he asked.

'Quite.'

'Try and help me tilt it then.'

'Don't change the subject. What am I getting that's so bad?'

'I don't know...,' he said.

'You don't know?'

'Maybe it isn't. I can't decide. Look I'm not a, I wasn't a... last night. I have before y'know. A lot.'

'Neither was I,' she said.

'Aye? And there's. Och well nothing serious but it's someone. Y'know cos I thought you weren't gonna, well...'

'How long's she been around?' she asked.

'About three months. *He's* been in Spain. Back now though.'

'Oh,' she said.

'See,' he said.

'What?' she said.

'I'm not a poof but. I know your lot hate that. I'm just, just...'

'Indecisive? Young, half-Jewish and bi?'

'Experimenting,' he said.

'So am I in the laboratory too? Got a checklist? What's next, goats?'

'Very funny.'

'Stitches.'

'I'm sorry.'

'Look. I'd better be getting back to work.'

She re-adjusted her headset, tucking back her immodest hair.

'You'll need a coke. Help you talk better,' he said.

'Better get one for yourself too.'

'Help me tilt it, eh?'

She sidled across the corridor and stretched her arms like a tart at a station. They each took hold of the smooth metal and swayed. The heavy machine began to oscillate and then rocked sideways, pinning his depravity against the wall. The sodomite pushed it off and it crashed level. Two cans dropped as stones from the slot. She picked up the first and handed it to her crumpled luti. Opening the other, she drank two slow gulps then turned away.

'I'll be seeing you,' she said.

He put the cold cylinder to his brow and slumped by the refreshment machine. His beautiful voice echoed down the short, dark corridor. My black-eyed lens, it wept with joy.

'What should we do?' he called to her departing back.

But she did not turn. She was not one of those who linger.

Author's Postscript: The gentleman who recounted to me this tale left our company soon afterwards to return to Cairo. He hides behind many fictions and I never heard from him again. The object of his confused jealousy later followed him. As for the woman, she is now my wife.

GMacN, Barcelona, December 2007

Putting yourself first

Margaret Callaghan

'Hi Ella, it's me. How are you?'

'I'm – '

'Oh good. I'm glad. I was worried when I hadn't heard from you.'

'How are you?' I asked. Penelope sighed. 'What's up?'

'Oh. It's just Simon, as ever. He wants to move back in. But I don't know if I want him to. Do I want to go back into the whole Noah's ark couple life? I mean he moved out once, he can do it again. And it's all that arguing over CDs and who bought what. It's so tedious. But then again I haven't met anyone better. I mean there's Robert of course, but he's really just an 'in-between' I think. His idea of foreplay is to tell me that his taxi is arriving in ten minutes. But I don't want to be single at 30. Can you imagine? I mean you're single of course but you're not 30 yet are you? And anyway it's different for you, you can cope with anything. You're so strong. I wish I could toughen up a little. It's just that I've always had a boyfriend I've just never had the luxury of being on my own. You know? Finding out what I want? You're so lucky. I mean we were so happy at first. Everyone wanted to be us. Everyone thought we were the perfect couple. And I could have got anyone in those days. I mean I used to walk into a party and choose who I wanted to leave with. But even if I met someone else I liked, how long do the good bits last anyway? Two years if you're lucky. Then it's back to arguing over whose turn it is to clean the kitchen or something.'

'You haven't seemed that happy with Simon for a while,' I interrupted.

'Hmm, maybe. But what's happiness anyway? It's ephemeral. It doesn't actually mean anything. I was reading this Buddhist book the other day and it said that you shouldn't seek happiness like a dog seeking a bone or something and that contentment was the key. And I was thinking it was so right. So maybe I should I just stick it out and aim for being content.'

'But weren't you worried that Simon might be gay?' I asked. I glanced at my watch. I had to leave in about five minutes and Penelope's calls were never short.

'Oh I don't think he is. What do you think? What does William think? He's got that gaydar thing. Can you ask him? I mean he says he isn't gay, Simon I mean, obviously William doesn't say he isn't gay. In fact, quite the opposite. He doesn't stop saying he's gay. Does he have to be gay *all the time*? I mean it's kind of been *done* hasn't it? It's quite nineties. I don't go round telling people I'm straight all the time. Anyway I asked him after you'd said that he might be and Simon said he just had that one fling at art school and everyone has an undergrad gay thing, don't they? How do you know unless you try? And you'll remember I snogged that girl in the LGBT society at Edinburgh? It was weird actually to have breasts pushed against me. I don't like breasts. Well not pushed against me. They're too soft. It's too odd. Actually Robert said I had the perfect breasts. I don't think I have. 32E is too large, I can't get anything to sit right and I'm always dropping crumbs down my cleavage and buttons are always opening up at the most inconvenient times. And men talk to them which is quite disconcerting. Especially when they're tall. It took me ages to realise. At first I just kept thinking everyone had a stoop or was shy or something. But anyway I was speaking to this guru woman and she said I've got to do what's right for me. And I realised that I never put myself first. So what do you think?'

'About you putting yourself first?' Penelope did little else, but I let her away with it. She was warm and friendly and if you were miserable she'd administer you champagne, pay you compliments and take you to a posh party. I only knew her vaguely when I moved through to Edinburgh, but she swept me up into her circle of friends and made sure I never felt lonely.

'Well, yes, well about Simon. Should I take him back?'

I thought of Simon's black silky hair and his air of patient amusement when Penelope was being particularly princessy. 'I don't know. You're a bit young to settle for 80 per cent, and Robert and you seem to be getting on pretty well.'

'I'm not sure that I think of Simon as being 80 per cent.'

'Don't you? Oh. I mean, he's a lovely guy of course,' I said.

'I think he's really attractive.'

'Oh, yeah. Of course.'

'Maybe you're right. Maybe I should give it a proper go with Robert. I think I'll ring Simon first though.'

'Right.'

'You think I shouldn't?' she asked.

'I think you should wait for him to ring you. Let him make the effort for once. If he doesn't ring you then you'll know he's not bothered.'

'Oh, right, maybe.'

'Well let me know how it goes. I'm going to have to rush off, I'm sorry,' I said.

'Okay, bye, darling. Thanks so much. You give such good advice.'

'Bye.' I hung up the phone.

I appraised myself in the mirror. More blusher, less lipstick, I decided. The natural look was the hardest. I pulled my hair into a knot, leaving a few strands around my face to make it look a little messy, sprayed on some perfume, grabbed my coat and skipped downstairs to the café below my flat.

He was waiting for me in a corner near the window. I watched him for a few moments before he saw me. His hair flopped over his eyes as he leaned forward to read the newspaper and I longed to reach over and brush it back from his face.

Just then he looked up and saw me. His face lit up.

'Oh hi Ella,' he said getting up to kiss me on the cheek and pull out a chair for me.

'Hi Simon,' I said sitting down.

'I'm sorry to drag you out like this and I know that you're friends with Penelope and won't want to betray her confidence, but you gave me such good advice before so er...' he began.

'It's fine,' I said, sitting on my hands to prevent myself from leaning forward and stroking his face.

'It's just that I'm wondering if maybe we should give it another go. She's got her faults but I love her, I think, and well–'

'You think?'

'Well, I'm fairly sure.'

'Right.'

'What?'

'Well,' I said, 'it's just that Penelope is such a good friend that I think she deserves to be with someone who really loves her, not someone who thinks that they do.'

'I guess. I hadn't thought of that.'

'And Robert is mad about her and–'

'Robert?' Simon interrupted. 'Is she seeing Robert?'

'Oh God, I'm sorry. Didn't you know? I would never have said anything if you didn't know.' I covered my mouth with my hand.

'It's not your fault, but she never said anything to me. Robert? He's one of my best friends.'

'Well, I'm sure she prefers you. Everyone says Robert is so attractive but I've never seen it myself. You're much more attractive.'

'Thanks.'

'And you did move out so she is free to see other people,' I went on.

'Yeah. I haven't though.'

'Well maybe you should. Maybe it's the best way to see if you're right for each other.'

'Maybe.' He looked worried.

'And of course there is the whole gay thing.'

'Gay thing?'

'Well, you know Penelope was seeing that girl at Edinburgh wasn't she?'

'I thought that was just a snog or something when she was drunk?'

'Oh. Is that what she said? Right. Okay. I must have misunderstood. That's probably what it was.'

'I think I'll phone her actually. It sounds like we have a lot to talk about.'

'Hmm. Maybe you should play hard to get a little. Penelope doesn't like guys who are too clingy.'

'Clingy? No. You're right. I'll wait until she rings me.'

'Listen, I've got to go, but if you want to meet for a drink on Friday we can talk about it some more? I'm sure it will all be fine in the end.'

'Right. Thanks Ella. I really appreciate it.'

'No problem,' I smiled.

10

Ulrich Hansen

01 – Thou shalt have no other gods before me
It had been one of a few places where she'd always wanted to take him. She'd felt it might help him understand who she was. It was her mother who'd taken her the first time. They had left Kabul in the morning and by the time they arrived it was cold and the sun had disappeared behind the mountains draining the landscape of its golden colours. Early next morning they had gone to see the two Buddhas. She had never been able to explain to him what it was she had felt there and now he would never find out. They kept showing the footage and she couldn't look away. It was taken with a hand-held camera and there was a slight jerk when the explosion came. The cloud of dust kept growing until eventually the wind moved it along, leaving just a dark cave where the sculpture once stood.

02 – Thou shalt not take the name of the LORD thy God in vain
'Best bacon ever,' she said smiling.

He folded the brown paper. Then he put an elastic band around it.

'It's organic,' he said, handing her the package.

He held the door for her as she left the shop. Half watching her as she got into her car, he rolled a cigarette, gave it a quick lick and lit it. As the paper caught fire a small flame flared up then died. He needed to clean the cold store; there would be more bodies coming tonight. He wondered how many more were left and what they would do to him when he was the last, the very last of his kind. Would they honour their oath like he'd honoured his? All he could do for now was go along with it. Refusing wouldn't get you off the hook, quite the contrary.

03 – Remember the Sabbath day, to keep it holy

Even from the shore it looked like the ugly boy in the class as it lay anchored among the sleek white sail boats. It weighed fifty tonnes, was made of iron and rigged with ill fitting Chinese sails. The owner and captain was Canadian, funding his stable diet of Mee Khong and raw fish by sailing tourists up and down the Strait of Malacca. He'd built the boat himself but he only told us once we were at sea. By then the hydraulics had failed and navigation was done with a wooden pole attached directly to the rudder. We were nine on-board. Five of us had volunteered to take shifts on those occasions where we would sail through the night. On the Saturday the wind worsened and during my midnight shift the rest of the boat was asleep. There was only the sound of the sea as it came against the boat and the gusts of wind making the sails flap. On the horizon lights from the fishing boats marked the border between the sea and the sky, but for a moment it felt as if it all came together.

04 – Honour thy father and thy mother

Politics was dangerous ground and me and my dad always avoided it. I never asked him directly but I knew his vote helped keep the government in power. They might not like foreigners, he would say, but if they don't want to work they shouldn't really be coming here, should they? And the economy is bet-ter than it's been for a long time. I once pointed out that Hitler turned the economy around as well. As an off the cuff remark he said that Hitler's real mistake was to start the war. Even though he wasn't born back then I could never look at those old photos quite the same way. All those happy faces, lit up in the night as they keep bringing more books to keep the fire going.

05 – Thou shalt not kill

She'd had it three years when it stopped eating. Mice, rabbits, it wouldn't touch anything. Initially the vet told her not to worry. Three weeks later she was back. Again he found nothing wrong with the animal. When he asked, she could think of no other changes in its behaviour. Only as she was about to leave, almost as an afterthought she'd told him. How in the morning when she woke, it used to lie at the foot of the bed curled up. Recently it had started making use of the space next to her stretching from one end of the bed to the other. Then he had asked her to sit down again. You need to get the animal destroyed immediately, he'd told her. It is measuring itself against you. It has stopped eating not because it is sick but because it is preparing itself for its big meal.

06 – Thou shalt not commit adultery
She is frozen. Around her the jeering crowd has come together. There is only a small open space for her to walk into, towards the photographer and into the photo. With nowhere to run to, the two uniformed men let her walk in front, while they follow a couple of steps behind. Her head is shaven and having nothing to hide behind she looks down. Was there in that bowing of her head an understanding of the part she played in this ritual or did she with that gesture take upon herself five years of collective anger? Or was she merely trying to understand how her love for a soldier could generate such hatred?

07 – Thou shalt not steal
Not be upset. Who were they to tell her not to be upset? That was for her and her only to decide and who said she was upset anyway? It was just the principle she didn't like because surely it was obvious to everyone that it had been her idea in the first place, even if no one had been listening. But no, of course not, but as soon as Ruth suggests putting some flowers up at the front then everybody thinks it is a fantastic idea. Well they could fill the whole damn place with flowers for all she cared, she for one would not be there to witness it, that was one thing they could be sure of.

08 – Thou shalt not bear false witness against thy neighbour
How he hated that question and how he hated the fact that almost every conversation seemed to lead there. Had they not all entered academia to formulate more exciting questions than that. When abroad he could get away with Scotland and in the UK he had even been to conferences where Glasgow would be fine. But most of the time there would be someone who knew Glasgow, one who wanted the details, one for whom Glasgow was never enough. And if he told them they would prod him for tales of urban warfare and gangland shootings, unemployed fathers and asthmatic mothers. But the worst was not when they asked. The worst was when there were no questions but just the narrowing of the eyes and the puzzlement. A puzzlement behind

which variations of the same question would linger even if not articulated, questions that he could never escape, but I thought that was a – and how he loathed that term – council estate.

09 – Thou shalt not covet thy neighbour's house
The entire village knew within a few hours. Judging by the crowd, I was one of the last to arrive and by then the helicopters had winched off the crew and disappeared. Not far out, sitting lopsided on the bank was the ship. With each wave washing over it more containers were pushed into the sea. Those that had already washed ashore were being emptied. Two men were carrying away a windscreen wrapped in protective film, another had a shiny exhaust pipe over his shoulder. Although no false lights were used to lure her in, I could not help feeling as we all stood there that as islanders we went back a long way and that this must have been what Stevenson called the harvest of the sea.

10 – Thou shalt not covet thy neighbour's wife
A strong leader, that was what was needed, not all these soft bureaucrats relying on think tanks and focus groups, afraid of telling the truth just because it was unpopular, no a real leader, like the ones they used to have, who would stand up and say the truth, that there were too many as it was, way too many of those foreigners, and if there were such a leader then he too would be prepared to do his part, and then finally without all of them flooding the place and stealing the women he too would find someone, yes, as a matter of fact they would be queuing up to be his wife, that he was quite sure of.

Bona fides

Sue Wilson

Karen had started taking evening classes a year or so after she got married, enrolling again the following autumn. With the Christmas break once more looming, she'd already had mulled wine and lotus dumplings this week with her Chinese Cookery group, and tonight her Art History for Beginners tutor, Don, was giving his end-of-term talk on famous forgers.

'Quite remarkable fidelity to the genuine article,' came his voice from behind her in the darkened room, as he clicked the PowerPoint along. 'Van Meegeren's Vermeers fooled all the leading experts of the day. He even passed one off to Göring during World War Two – and then afterwards had to admit it was a fake, otherwise he'd have been charged with treason, for selling national treasures to the Nazis. They didn't believe him at first, so he ended up painting another Vermeer in prison, to prove he really was that good.'

Karen thought what she felt for Don – and maybe he for her – could have been real. But she'd never know now. Mike had certainly been adamant about that. His indefinite leave to remain had come through no problem, over a month ago now, but their deal had been three years, just to be safe, and he wasn't prepared to take any chances. Besides, as he'd said reasonably after she'd conceded, and he'd got her a beer from the fridge, even if she was will-ing to be totally hush-hush about it, what guy was going to be up for all that, all so her 'husband' could stay in the country?

'Alongside Myatt's skill as a forger,' Don was saying now, 'Drewe was an absolute genius at creating a phony paper trail, all the umpteen layers of documentation you need nowadays to prove authenticity.'

Karen had become quite an expert in that herself. Having plighted their bargain, she and Mike had begun their 'romance' planning out the details in various plush restaurants and cosy bars, before laying further groundwork with city breaks and country-house hotels. Given what was left on his original visa, he'd figured six months should be enough. He'd used up most of the time he was allowed to work, but had earned plenty to splurge on a whirlwind courtship, meanwhile busily planning the business he'd be allowed to set up after the wedding.

You will be required to supply information and/or documentary evidence about when, where and how you and your fiancé(e) met... and/or any additional supporting evidence about your relationship which might help your application.

Karen had looked everything up in internet cafés: computers being Mike's game, he knew all about traceability. There'd been a lot of excitement, those first few months: partners in crime, plotting their perfect scam – all those smiling photos looked very convincing. As she'd secretly basked in the unfamiliar absence of financial anxiety, her friends had enviously teased her new-found soppiness: saving the cards and notes he showered her with, storing his emails and texts in their own special files.

Wilfully making a material statement which you know to be false is a serious offence, carrying a maximum penalty of seven years imprisonment or a fine.

Only Hazel, Karen's very oldest, closest friend, and Mike's business partner Craig knew the truth. That had been one of Mike's deal-breakers – and she'd had to dig her heels in hard for Hazel, her winning argument ultimately that their secret would be safer that way. Even though sometimes now it seemed it would have been easier just to have lied to everyone and had done with it.

Mike would be angry enough if he knew that on the first night of Introductory Spanish last year, in the car park before going in, as before every class since, she'd taken off her rings. She'd reasoned that if anyone was there who even might possibly come to know of her or Mike, she'd just make sure and wear them after that, but so far no one had been. None of her groups had proved very sociable outwith their allotted time, and she'd gone along with the general hanging back. It had just been a kind of secret respite, without any elaborate falsehood, to excise Mike from such outline information as she gave, and at least pretend she was being herself.

As had become usual, Don joined her outside for a cigarette at the half-way break, sheltering in the doorway against a bitter wind. She was already feeling distant and wistful about him, but he was too buzzed to notice her forlornly averted eyes and indrawn shoulders. He was writing a book about forgers and fakes: from what she'd gathered it wasn't actually much past the proposal stage, but he was bullish about its prospects.

'There's just so many layers to the whole thing,' he enthused again now, as Karen pined for the pale skin she'd never touch, the bony gesturing fingers that would never touch her. 'A lot of these guys, the really good ones, they do their time when they get caught, and then afterwards they make a shedload more money selling more fakes, only now it's all up front. I was looking up stuff on Tony Tetro the other day, and it said – I memorised the phrase, it was so fantastic – 'He currently executes master copies for an exclusive list of elite clients from his studio in Southern California.' How cool is that? I mean, how fucking twenty-first century is that?'

Karen had initially supposed she and Mike might end up getting it on occasionally, along the line. They'd begun with an easy rapport, a lot of shared humour, yet without any serious flirtatious intent: that was partly why he'd approached her in the first place. They weren't each other's type, but neither considered the other unattractive. Given how anything extra-marital was *verboten*, she'd just kind of thought maybe sometimes they'd end up more than technically in bed together, just in a friendly sort of way.

But the thrill of adventure had ended abruptly at the wedding, as she handed Hazel her flowers to start the ceremony and glimpsed the pity in her best friend's eyes. Not even a moment of truth, only the merest instant before Karen looked away, safely back in character – until she lay wide-eyed beside a snoring Mike in the honeymoon suite that night, he still in most of his suit, she in pyjamas, and let herself admit, for a moment, truly what she'd done. She'd never imagined finding it so hard to say the actual words, to have them so trustingly witnessed. Then she made herself think about the money, how if she wasn't lying here she'd be wide awake in her old flat, worrying about her debts. This way she was free and clear before she was thirty – and on a pretty cushy number in the meantime. Besides, it was too late to back out now.

'So if a fake's good enough to fool the experts, does it actually matter that it's a fake? If a painting ticks all the same artistic and aesthetic boxes as the so-called real thing, why should it matter?'

After the break, Don had brought out wine and paper cups, had them rearrange the chairs into a circle, and attempted to initiate a discussion. He said it would give them an interesting angle on some of the underlying issues involved in what they were looking at.

'Surely it's to do with soul,' said Margaret, a middle-aged lady who dabbled equally in adult education and New Age enlightenment now that her children had left home. 'With the real thing, the real artist will have put a little bit of their soul into it, and that's what can't be faked. That's what makes something precious.'

Apart from Karen, only three others took up Don's suggestion of another drink afterwards, and only she accepted his offer of a second, the rest departing in a flurry of polite festive wishes. She felt she owed herself this one longing taste of being properly alone with him, before gritting her teeth and getting back to reality.

He'd been across the table from her, but when he eventually returned from the bar he sat in close alongside, turning to clink glasses as he draped his other arm along the top of the booth behind. She smiled back, trying to edge away, but his hand grasped her shoulder, pulling her against him. She could smell the cigarette he'd nipped outside for, felt the wine she'd gulped suddenly curdling, sour and queasy in her empty stomach.

'So here we are at last,' he said. 'It's taken long enough – you were forever rushing off – but we got here in the end.'

'What do you mean?'

'Oh, come on,' he said, widening his gorgeous twinkly grin. 'What's all the big eye contact and meaningful chat been about all term? It certainly wasn't just me doing that.'

'No, I'm sorry – I mean, I'm married.'

He shrugged. 'Me too. I thought you might be. Two can play at the rings game, you know. Anyway, I'm not talking about anything serious.'

The rush of disgust sent her stumbling to the Ladies, bent her retching over the toilet, although nothing came up. Eventually, she rinsed her mouth, splashed her face, then looked in the mirror, trying not to see what he'd seen.

The crossword

Lucy Adams

Enough was enough. As she lay there waiting for the flick-flack of *The Times* being forced through the letterbox, she decided. Today she would cancel the paper. Jimmy had been dead twelve years almost to the day and there was no space left. Their home looked like a recycling dump, a museum piece. The bedroom was the only room unfettered by glaring headlines. There was a dull thud as the paper dropped to the mat. It was the sign to pull back the covers and swing her numb legs to the floor. Josephine wished she had some sort of a machine to dress her. She held the side of the bed and prepared her legs to take her weight. As the blood rushed down to her feet the ache was unbearable, like the throbbing pain after particularly bad pins and needles, but worse. She twisted the radio's 'on' dial and Classic FM began in the middle of a piece.

Sitting in the plastic chair ordered for her after the last fall, she washed behind her neck and under her armpits with a flannel. Always the same order, always the same cold pain, as the night's stiffness hung in her bones. Socks were the hardest so that's what she started with. She'd need two pairs today. Holding the side of the chair with an arthritic hand she bent forwards slowly. Once she was steady enough she used her hooked index fingers to draw the sock towards her ankle. Easy, she thought as she inhaled deeply, resisting the urge to slump forwards. Next came the trousers. Today it would take a little longer than usual to get ready. She was going out and out was somewhere she had not been for quite some time.

She was so absorbed in dressing that she jumped when the doorbell rang.

'Josephine?'

'Yes.' Her voice was barely audible. She felt a little disorientated. No one had asked for her for a while.

'Is that you? It's Della from next door. You sound a little queer?'

Josephine slotted her dental plate into position and pushed herself up from the armrests. Her skin looked almost translucent in the mirror, like the baking paper she'd lined her once-famous fruitcakes in. She could only see the lipstick she used for evenings. It was far too dark but it would have to do.

She had to shout for her voice to carry down the hall.

'Oh hello, dear. I'm fine, thank you. Quite fine.'

She knew that Della had promised to check in on her from time to time, but she couldn't let anyone see the state of the place.

'Are you coming to the door dear? It's awfully cold out.'

Perhaps if she just opened the door on the latch; that would prove satisfactory as a check-up.

'I was just a little worried,' Della said, her mouth close to the letterbox, her body bent over and distorted by the frosted glass door. 'I haven't seen you for a while and this morning I noticed your curtains were drawn. They're still drawn in fact.'

'I'm just coming.'

Getting to the door was never easy. Josephine surveyed the piles of crinkled, yellowing papers ahead of her along the hallway. The carpet was only visible as a narrow strip, a jagged canyon boxed off with square edges as tall as the radiator. Placing her right hand on the wall for support she pointed her toe and edged it into a gap only wide enough for one foot at a time. She breathed in and a sharp pulse shot down her leg as it took her weight.

'Hang on, Della.'

Jimmy had read *The Times* every day from cover to cover since she could remember. Even when they'd gone to the beach at Eastbourne that first time, and he'd held her hand as they walked, the shingle squeezing up between their toes. She remembered seeing it too by the hospital bed after the miscarriage and how its familiarity had comforted her. He would even read the advertisements. And in the evenings, sitting close enough on the moss-green sofa that she could feel the warmth from his leg, they'd done the crossword together, line by line.

'Yesterday's news is not tomorrow's chip wrapper,' he'd say to her in that earnest way he had, pointing his finger towards the blank television in the corner or the bookshelf, as if there were an audience. 'It's a fragment of history and the bedrock of today's news. It's an anchor. We forget the past or lose hold of the what's going on day to day and we'd be lost. Lost.'

Josephine didn't want to feel lost, but the multifarious supplements these days meant she didn't have time to read it all and over the course of the week the different sections accrued in different parts of the lounge and hall, piled on top of last week's, last month's. She tried not to think about them decaying there, the pages going brittle and yellow with time, old dead things as useless now as the trees which made them. What had been one box in the corner, was now taking over the house. His view was that a paper should only be discarded once you had read it all and completed the main crossword. Since he'd gone she'd struggled to get through all of the news pages. By the time she reached the crossword she was too tired. Even with his thesaurus and dictionary propped up next to her, she could seldom answer more than two or three clues. Last night's effort had been the worst to date. The clues were still jostling for space in her mind. She had failed to fill in even the easy ones.

'Josephine?'

She had to concentrate. The pile on the right looked particularly precarious and her hips were a little too wide. Standing so close to them she noticed, as if for the first time, that they gave off a faint smell of cat pee.

'Coming, Della. Sorry. I'm just a little slow in the mornings.'

She felt light-headed and stopped, resting her hand on a story about *The Hutton Report*. The date and all the details were right there so she didn't have to remember. Quite a convenient library, she thought and chuckled. She couldn't even remember what she'd had for dinner the night before. Perhaps she'd skipped it. She wasn't much hungry this week.

She edged her way to the door and opened it as far as the metal chain would allow.

'Della. How sweet of you to pop round. It's just not very convenient right now.'

'Well I saw the curtains and I...'

'Oh yes. I like to leave them drawn when I'm going out into town. So people think someone's in.'

'But it's awfully cold out. If there's something you need couldn't you let me get it for you?'

Having to rely on others, Jimmy had said, was the end. If you couldn't look after yourself there was no point. Josephine was so glad that he'd passed away at home while he still had his wits about him, but couldn't help the fact that sometimes she felt bitterness and jealousy that he'd gone without her. It crept under her skin, like the tiny shards of glass you couldn't see or sweep up after a breakage. Some days, she resented his absence as much as the mountain of newspapers that had taken his place.

'Josephine, are you all right, dear?'

'Oh yes, dear. Completely. Well as much as I'll ever be. And it's kind of you to offer but really there's no need. I'll be just fine. The exercise will do me good anyway.'

'Well just let me know, won't you.' Della didn't sound quite sure about letting it be. It was just like her, terribly kind, but slightly overbearing.

'Yes, of course. And thank you for coming over.'

Josephine picked up today's newspaper from the mat and began to navigate back through the hall. She spent longer than usual over her cornflakes and turned each page of the paper tentatively smoothing it down, as if it were a precious relic. The rain had stopped. It was time to go outside, but she didn't know if she was up to it. It took another hour to choose which gloves to wear and to find the right shopping bag. She checked and double checked her purse then turned off all the electric sockets, just in case. She would wear his tartan scarf. Sometimes from the older clothes she would still get a faint waft of his smell. She covered her face with it, but no. It was just fusty.

As she opened the door the cold forced her to step backwards. The sky was milky and soft looking. The air stung her cheeks. Just one step at a time, that's how all tasks were achieved. She looked left and right, surveying the status of the other homes in the close, knowing at a glance who was in. She stared down at the welcome mat. It was too cold. Her right hand was shaking visibly now as she tried to button her coat. Buttons and bra straps were the worst. Then it came to her. Last night's first clue: four down, denigration. She would need to write that down before she forgot. She clutched the wooden frame as she turned around slowly and closed the door behind her.

Brief encounters

Fiona Montgomery

Susie found her seat and sat down, anticipating hours of uninterrupted pleasure thanks to the new book in her bag.

Within minutes she was drinking in the first chapter, only vaguely conscious of the carriage filling up before the engine juddered and the train pulled slowly out of Glasgow.

'Susie McKenna? Is that you?'

She didn't recognise the voice, but her stomach lurched when she saw the woman, about her own age, cropped auburn hair, laden with bags and a steaming coffee.

'Oh! Laura, hi!' she managed, dropping the book.

Laura seemed flustered too, but for different reasons. 'I nearly missed the bloody train. I think that's my seat, up at the end there.' She glanced down at the empty space beside Susie, the reservation ticket above it saying *Crewe – London Euston*, then at the hardback on the table.

'You're reading. I won't interrupt, but let's catch up later, perhaps over lunch? When did we last see each other? Gordon's surprise fortieth? That must be four, five years ago?'

'Four years,' Susie said, feeling nauseous.

She'd deliberately not invited Laura to the fortieth, but she'd turned up in a crowd of latecomers from their student days, most of whom were welcome.

Laura smiled and left, waving goodbye.

'How lovely to see an old friend on a long, boring journey,' said the elderly woman opposite. Susie picked the book up, not wanting to encourage conversation by answering. The words were all blurred. She wiped her eyes.

Palpitations followed the tears. Susie struggled to slow her breathing and mentally scolded herself, pointing out she had time to think about this. Laura wasn't expecting her to be any different than on previous occasions. She'd always been polite and could keep up that façade. Yet...

She contemplated the options, including inviting Laura to sit beside her. But all the way to Crewe – or worse, to London? What a nightmare. She could just read on, but Laura mentioned lunch, so would no doubt be back. Anyway, how could she concentrate on the book now? Leave at Motherwell and get the next train? Great idea, Susie thought, relieved. Chicken, said her inner voice, which she'd recently learned to trust.

Taking a deep breath, Susie manoeuvred into the aisle and headed along, holding onto the tops of seats as the train gathered speed. Laura looked up, surprised.

Susie croaked, 'I'm going to the buffet car for a coffee. Would you like to come? We could do that catching up.'

Laura shook the cardboard mug, testing how much was left. She seemed about to decline, then smiled. 'You can never have too much caffeine.'

They started off, with Susie hoping there'd be a less crowded section on the way. Possibly not the designated quiet carriage though. Causing a scene there could spark complaints to Virgin and God knows what further ignominies.

Spotting an empty table, she suggested that Laura claim it while she went for the drinks. Five minutes later she returned and sat facing Laura, despite an aversion to travelling backwards. She could hardly ask to swap seats. Stirring sugar into the coffee, she was ready to counter the expected small talk.

'What ages are your boys now?' Laura ventured.

'Twenty and 18. But I didn't ask you here to talk about them. I am touched by your interest though, given the way you behaved when I was pregnant with Jamie.'

Susie felt unexpectedly proud of herself, going right to the heart of things. Her broken heart, back then.

Laura put her cup down and looked around. 'I don't know what you mean,' she said, turning pale.

'You know. You lied at the time. And I stupidly believed you both.'

'I really don't want to have this conversation,' Laura said, moving to stand up, presumably looking for a dignified exit.

'Fucking sit down and admit I've got every right to be mad,' Susie hissed, causing a few people to look over from nearby seats.

Laura sat abruptly. 'I don't understand. It must be 20 years ago...'

'What was 20 years ago? Remind me.' Susie disturbed herself with the bitterness in her voice. Very undignified. She tried to rein it back. 'We both need this conversation. I'm sure you feel bad.'

'I've got nothing to feel guilty for, actually. I wasn't cheating on anyone. Gordon was.'

Susie couldn't help letting out an audible sigh. The relief seemed perverse, but despite Gordon's confession during couples counselling two years ago, she still hadn't been sure he'd told the whole truth. She sometimes wondered whether he was capable of admitting something he'd not done, to punish her for going on about things. Hopefully, Laura's answer would put her paranoia to rest.

'Why now, after all these years?' asked Laura. 'You've been nice enough before.'

'I stupidly gave you both the benefit of the doubt,' Susie replied. 'I thought perhaps he really was comforting you because you were upset.' Her voice trembled. 'But he admitted recently that you two did have sex. While I was downstairs! I hate you both for that and for all the lies.'

Ever since the counselling ended, she'd imagined bumping into Laura, knowing she would have to say something. She'd not pictured it like this, with a train full of strangers to witness her pain.

Suddenly she was back there, bursting in to find the father of her baby with his arm round Laura, sitting on a double bed at one of the post-finals parties. A bulging eight months pregnant, she had been chatting in the kitchen when she realised how long Gordon had been away and went looking for him.

'What the hell are you doing?' she yelled at Gordon, before running to the bathroom and locking herself in.

He hammered on the door for what seemed like hours, while she alternately listened to his pleading, then screamed to be left alone. At one stage Laura said through the door, 'Susie, you've got the wrong end of the stick. Nothing happened.'

'I hate you,' she repeated over and over, her voice becoming more hoarse as she wondered if she'd over-reacted. Who did she hate? Gordon, Laura, or her pathetic, insecure self?

The drama broke up the party. Gordon eventually persuaded her to come out. 'I love you,' he said, when she undid the lock, mascara streaked across her face. 'It's not what you think. I promise. Come on home, Susie.'

Safe in their bed, he'd held her close and insisted that Laura was crying over an ex, had simply needed a cuddle.

She'd tried to believe that for 18 years. But the counsellor saw how the incident had hovered in the background throughout their marriage, setting a tone of sorts. Susie never felt sure she could believe him, over that or later issues between them. Gaslighting was the term, fucking with your mind, so you could no longer tell what was real. At least Gordon had finally owned up. Now Laura had confirmed it.

She looked into the other woman's eyes and spoke slowly, wanting an answer to this too. Laura couldn't evade all responsibility.

'I was about to give birth. What kind of a person are you?'

Laura crumpled, sobbing. Susie sensed people nearby trying to act as if they weren't listening to every word. Why the fuck the tears? She didn't want to feel sympathy.

'I was in the wrong. And I'm glad you two stayed together.'

It was said through sniffles and Susie instinctively reached in her bag for a tissue.

Laura blew her nose, then spoke in a whisper. 'I assumed you believed us that nothing happened. Sometimes that's best. You don't realise what I'd gone through.'

Susie leant forward, about to explode. But something stopped her. She waited.

'I got pregnant the year before finals and he didn't want to know...'

Susie remembered talk of an operation. 'You told everyone you had your appendix out.'

Laura nodded and continued. No one but Susie could hear. 'Mum, Dad, my friends... they all talked me into having an abortion. I really didn't want to.' She was sobbing again, uncontrollably now.

Susie reached to touch her hand and sat waiting.

Eventually Laura wiped her face and looked up. 'I'm so sorry. I think it was because he and you had everything I'd just lost. I loved being in his arms and it went on from there. I didn't think about how much it would hurt you.'

Susie felt numb. Was this apology genuine, more so than her husband's?

'Did Gordon tell you why?' Laura asked.

'He claimed it was a moment of weakness. Being drunk. He just gave in to what was on offer, then didn't dare admit it to me.'

'That's not what I meant,' said Laura. 'Did he tell you why I was upset? About the abortion?' Her voice was urgent. 'He promised me he wouldn't.'

Susie's heart hurt, but she said quietly, 'He kept his promise.'

Scar tissue

E J Patience

When my cousin Marla was nine her father raped a woman.

Marla had been crouching behind the bed in a feeding frenzy of cracker crumbs and clawing chunks of Edam when she heard their inebriated ascent of the stairs. She made quickly for the wardrobe, dropping the knife in haste to conceal her crime. A premeditated crime as she had chosen the spare room for the very reason that she would have more warning of intruders from there.

As she hid in the mothy darkness with the cheese that she had stolen from the buffet and the sounds of the eighties hammering away beneath her feet, she listened. She heard their drunken coupling turn to a struggle as the woman changed her mind and began to protest and struggle. Then there was a scream. Her father's laughter changed to a surprised gasp as he collapsed with a loud groan.

There were no witnesses to the stabbing. Marla heard the woman making her way breathlessly downstairs in great sobbing lurches. That was when Marla made her escape. She ran from the room, torn between fear and love with no time to pass judgement or stop for grief. There were no witnesses at all. Marla couldn't risk her mother finding out about the cheese. It would mean another week of lettuce and clear soup.

'You'll never have a nice figure when you grow up if you stuff yourself like that.' And then Marla would have to come round and beg from my mother, but now Marla guessed Aunty Chrissy would be so sad about her murdered brother that she wouldn't feel sorry for Marla any more.

Marla knew what she had to do. Like all good criminals she disposed of the evidence, on this occasion, down the toilet. She watched ruefully as the half-digested food churned briefly before disappearing forever and she wiped her mouth with a tissue.

Marla didn't know that it was Mrs Shapiro until the next day when she heard a neighbour telling the postman that she wasn't surprised. Not surprised at all, given that Mrs Shapiro was how she was. None of the women liked her, although they pretended to – all of the men had loved her. The postman wondered how difficult it must have been to inflict that much damage with only a cheese knife, especially if they had both been so pissed.

He was told, 'She got him in an artery in his neck, and in his lung too or so I've been told.' Marla didn't want to listen any more.

Back then, before the stabbing, I used to call in for Marla so we could walk to school together. Each morning we would watch Mrs Shapiro waft past us to her car, a perfumed presence. Marla and I would dream of looking just like her when we finally developed breasts, and we assumed that the sensuous gash of lipstick and the eyes so dark they were almost black would come naturally as part of the metamorphosis.

Marla's mother was a confused and selfish wretch who had been screwed up right from the start. A woman who imposed her own crazed ideas and impossible standards on her daughter right up until what my own mother called 'the incident.' After that, Marla's mum could no longer cope so Marla came to live with us when she was ten. We were raised as sisters, but in all that time I always felt that I never really knew her. How could I? We knew nothing of what Marla had witnessed.

By the time Marla was sixteen she had given up visiting her mother. There was only so much pity in her for a woman who could not love and gave nothing.

We didn't know.

She would head off at the same time every week, but her visits were no longer to her mother's house. It wasn't until many years later, when she told me the whole story, that I realised where she had been going. She told me that the prison had always smelled bad, that it reeked of boiled meat and the smell would make her wretch, but there was such a compulsion to attend. She spoke of the last time she had been there and how Doris Shapiro had sounded almost relieved as she said, 'You can't visit me here any more. I'm going to a re-hab centre.' Marla said that her eyes had faded to a dull brown and without the lipstick, her mouth had seemed lost and without direction. It would be eight years before Marla saw Doris Shapiro again.

By the time we were adults, I'd given up trying to understand her.

'You'll die before you're thirty if you carry on abusing yourself like this,' I told her. People thought she was my baby sister. We were equal in years but Marla's body was stunted, retarded in growth by starvation. Marla was clever. She knew exactly how much weight she could drop without being hospitalised, which was too much, but enough to keep her alive and functioning, just.

My mother was beside herself, desperate to nurture her brother's child. The last remnant of her beloved sibling. Marla knew it. It wasn't something my mother could hide. She tried not to plead but like me, Marla could see it in the way she turned her face just as the plate touched the table. It was in all of her. Sometimes I hated Marla for what she was doing to my mother. Every tiny action of every single day was another opportunity for Marla to cause a little more hurt to the one person she knew she could wound. I remember watching as the light faded in my mother's eyes one day while we chatted to someone in the street. People always thought Marla was still a child.

'Are you going to help Mum at the shops?' And, 'You can pat her if you like, love. She's very friendly'

Marla was merciless. She looked up with those cold blue eyes. Sunken pebbles lost in the translucent, downy skin.

'I'm 23," she said in her nine year-old's voice. 'I'm 23 with a law degree and anorexia. You pat the fucking dog.'

My own mother blamed her estranged sister-in-law for so much that we ourselves had no contact with her for years. It was something of a relief when we discovered that Marla had stopped going round there. As a child I had heard the same diatribe so many times that I knew it by heart.

'I don't know why he ever married her. She never loved him you know...or Marla. What man wouldn't look elsewhere....and him such a good father? He loved Marla so much...'

It was true. Marla had been close to her father and they adored each other. He was her beacon in the ocean of neglect that filled the house when Marla was alone with her mother.

I never guessed that Marla had managed to track down Doris Shapiro once more. When Marla started going out regularly on a Tuesday night I worried that she was back in contact with her mother, although I had a vague hope that she might be doing something normal like meeting friends or even a man.

My mother begged me to follow her and so one night I stood in a deserted alleyway, watching Marla approach a small, damp terraced house. She knocked three times and Doris opened the door. I moved closer and was able to see them through the kitchen window. They hardly spoke a word. Marla took off her coat and laid it over a chair, then waited while Doris flooded the centre of the room with light. Lamps, angle poise reading lights, even torches, all trained to the centre of the room where Marla stood. I began to realise that I was watching a ritual that had been repeated many times.

Marla undid her blouse and allowed it to fall to the floor. Doris Shapiro circled her slowly like an art critic, unable to remove her eyes from the emaciated, skeletal form of my cousin. Her eyes roamed greedily over the protruding ribcage and non-existent breasts. She stepped back and squinted at a hollow in the neck, moved in closer to peer at a wing-like shoulder blade, touched a little, then went around the room again, re-adjusting the lights for better illumination of a certain spot. And all the time, her face was a mixture of disgust, fascination and satisfaction.

Sickened, yet mesmerised, I continued to watch as Doris changed places with Marla. Modestly, she pulled up her jumper and took it off over her head. I noticed how matted her hair had become as she pulled the long greying mass forwards and off her shoulders.

Silver, glistening scar tissue swam up her back like a shoal of herring. Some of the wounds were new and blossomed in pink and red blooms as the marks of self-flagellation matured.

From the desk of Judy

A Singerman

I've decided to share my secret.

I have no ears. You wouldn't realise if you saw me because a doctor transplanted a pair on the sides of my head. They don't work, obviously, which is why I said I have no ears, but they're a real pair; they belonged to a great aunt of mine behind whose ~~face~~ back my mother used to make crazy expressions because this aunt had had all these different boyfriends (sorry, gentleman companions) but never married. I remember how the ears smelt of her thick, dusty make-up. I couldn't stop sneezing.

Where was I? These thoughts of my great aunt distracted me from the serious point I'm trying to make, I mean, communicate. I can't hear any sound but I'm incredibly adept at reading lips and I tell people I have a funny voice because I swallowed a pair of nail-scissors when I was young which made drastic alterations to my vocal cords. Most people believe it as they've no reason to doubt me. But my girlfriend, I couldn't keep it from her.

I tried to. Early on it was easy, we sat facing each other in restaurants and I told her I liked to concentrate on the film when I'm at the cinema. To be frank, I'm probably a better listener than most people because of the effort required on my part. But there's one thing I couldn't handle: whispering in my ear.

Judy and I had slept together a few times before she finally said it.

'Why are you so silent?' she asked, her head resting on her hand, elbow dug into the pillow.

'What do you mean? I'm talking aren't I?'

'In bed. You never respond to anything I say.'

'I think silence is romantic,' I said, pulling her closer and pushing my lips against hers...

Breathless, I dropped my head on the pillow and faced the ceiling. Judy got up, sat on my chest, legs enclosing my arms, and looked down at me.

'You're deaf, aren't you?' she said, smiling.

'Why do you say that?' I asked. Another crack had formed in the plaster above the bed.

'I told you I used to be a man and you didn't even react.'

She caught me so I let it out, how I wasn't deaf but was born in a rare condition with the ears omitted. I even told her the origins of my pair. Judy laughed and said she'd thought they smelled funny.

Then it was Judy's turn. I watched those lips tell of youthful confusion: the preference for the ~~blue oops~~ pink bicycle, the fistfights, the boyfriends.

'One day the perfect opportunity arose,' said Judy. 'My Uncle Pete was in a serious car crash and his penis was severed. Most people would be grateful just to remain breathing but no, not our Pete. He happened to consider himself the greatest hit with the ladies since Champion Phil Tuxedo. (Don't ask. Pete was delusional.) So I went into the surgery and happily sacrificed my member for Uncle Pete. I stepped out the hospital a woman and he swaggered through the doors with my cock between his legs.'

'Did it work?'

'What?'

'You know, the new apparatus?'

'Oh, could he go stiff? No, I don't think so, but it reassured him to know that there was something down there.'

It was like we were made for each other. The foundation of our relationship was not honesty, nor was it mutual trust; Judy and I were a perfect couple because we deliberately accepted appearances as reality. She was a woman and I could hear her voice.

I could also smell the other men on her but she never mentioned them and I never saw them so it didn't matter to me at all. Not even the little, slightest bit. I believed she loved me because she acted like she did. She, on the other hand, wanted me to act like I didn't love her. I pretended to hate her, locking her out the flat, hiding her lingerie, blackening her eye, that sort of thing. This made Judy act like she loved me even more, which I adored, but ignored. Everything was working extremely well.

Then, one day, there was a knock on my door. I opened it and saw a man on the doorstep.

'Ta-DA!'

'Excuse me, do I know you?'

'It's me,' he said, 'Judy.'

'You're not Judy,' I said.

'Uncle Pete died last week and left me his ... my ... our penis in his will. I told you I was getting the operation today.'

'You didn't tell me that!' I held onto the door frame for balance.

'Yes I did. I whispered it in your ear while we were fucking last night.'

I was speechless.

I tried to get used to the new Judy, but it wasn't the same. It was hard to get rid of him at first because the more I said I hated him and punched him and threw his new clothes through the windows onto the soggy grass three floors below, the more he loved me. Eventually I knew what I had to do.

'Judy, I love you.'

He shifted on the sofa. His legs crossed.

'I mean it, Judy,' I said, moving closer and fixing my eyes on his grey-blue irises. 'With all my heart, I love you.'

He got up and, as I screamed my undying affection at him in a crescendo of three stretched-out roaring syllables, ran from the room, the flat, the building; I stuck my head out the window and laughed as ~~Tom~~ Judy sprinted down the street like a cheetah chasing after its lost spots.

'I won't be hearing from you again,' I shouted and laughed even harder at my own wit.

To be honest, I'm at my wit's end now. I got bored and lonely and came up with this to make myself feel better. It didn't work. Too much goes wrong. I'm vague when losing control. Did Judy really accept appearances as reality? She was meant to, but she became complicated. I'm not sure I understood her. Maybe she did want loved, but too late. It's hard to say.

I wanted to imagine having no ears and I wanted you to believe me. But there's so much to think about and the mind races beyond. I've been meaning to ask: is an ear an ear if it cannot hear? Must something function to be? It depends on what you believe.

I have a lot of questions. I wanted to know why Judy cheated on me, why she changed. But did she change, or was she just pretending to love me all along? I meant it when I said NO! I mean wrote. I meant it when I wrote it was like we were mad for each other. Who knows who made us, but we were

Real life is quite frightening, I find. Especially the way you think you understand what you're doing, believe you have it all held tight in your hands, then suddenly, in a single moment, just the time it takes to step into your bedroom on a Wednesday afternoon and scream 'Tom, what the hell are you doing here?', you see it all differently.

Everything looks different now. I step over the body (her?) to get a good look at myself in the mirror. I'm thin so they fit me all right but the panties looked better on Judy. They used to be milky-white printed with perfect little sunflowers. I'm sorry I made a mess.

There are many things that could be explained but I prefer to pose questions because there are no answers. People find it harder to catch you for your mistakes this way. Is there no answer?

I meant it when I said I have no ears. I do have ears, but it's quiet in here; there's no silence, but it's so quiet. I might have lost my head. Tom's gone. I never trusted him, I knew it, but he can't have phoned the police. Yet. That's good, I wanted us to think for a while. I can't hear you and you will only get this from me. There are great distances in relationships. Things get confusing, mixed-up, complicated. We both know this was a twisted fantasy. The key is understanding it takes faith to commit.

Are you listening? I'm trying to say goodbye.

Our little joke

Helen Sedgwick

Lucy was lying in bed. Unable to stay still. Turning onto her side, bending and stretching her legs, all the while straining to hear the noises that kept coming from Katrina's bedroom next door.

Why was Katrina doing this? Why had she brought him home, let him touch her? It didn't make sense.

On the walk home that night Katrina had made Lucy follow. Katrina and Steve in front, Lucy behind. Watching as Steve put his hand on Katrina's back, inside her jacket. As it moved lower. As he forced it into the back pocket of Katrina's jeans. His knuckles wouldn't fit. They were too prominent for the tightly cut black denim. The picture of it was fresh, still, in Lucy's mind. From several paces behind them she had stared at his hand. At his fingers cut off at the knuckles, at his wrist bent awkwardly, and had thought of a broken limb, bent sharp, fractured bones splintering.

She had enjoyed the thought.

But then Katrina had turned and said something quietly in Steve's ear. Lucy couldn't hear what was said, but she saw them smile and pull in closer together. Lucy hated the feeling, but knew at once that she couldn't turn away until Katrina spoke again. That's what she was waiting for now. She had to hear it. All of it. She had to hear everything that was going on in Katrina's room.

Lucy breathed slowly. Got up, out of bed, and walked over to the far wall. She pushed some of her CDs out of the way, which were stacked up in ordered piles, alphabetised, all around the edges of her bedroom. Quietly. She cleared enough room to sit sideways, shivering, her left ear pressing against the wall, her legs bent, knees hugged into her chest.

She could hear Steve's laughter.

Something malicious in it, she thought. He was laughing at her. Gloating. She was sure of it. What had Katrina said to pull that laugh out of him? She spoke quietly, Katrina. Forcefully but quietly. Her voice wouldn't transmit, not unless she wanted it to.

It was dark in Lucy's bedroom, the only lights coming from the face of the alarm clock and the street lights outside. The ceiling was high, the lack of furniture dictating that all Lucy's possessions be arrayed on the floor. She looked up, trying to think clearly, to focus on the vast unavailable space that composed the top half of her bedroom. There was a spider's web in the corner, old and dusty, black looking instead of white or transparent. It had spread all around the cornice work. Beautiful twirls and fine details of plaster filled in with blackened silky webs, matted now, half eaten and torn; the final resting place of the insects.

Lucy heard a crash in the room beyond the wall.

Straining to hear. It sounded like a glass had smashed. And now she was imagining the glass splintering, sharp shards splayed around the point of impact, blood drops, red and dark and rich. She could hear his voice, muttering an apology, made clumsy and insincere by alcohol. 'Kat,' he said. Why was he calling her Kat? Her name was Katrina. Lucy called her Katrina. But maybe she liked Kat better? Lucy listened, grinding her teeth. She couldn't move, couldn't get away. She had to hear. Needed to be a part of it.

But not in a bad way.

She raised herself onto her knees, reaching towards the bed. Almost falling, grabbing a corner, pulling roughly. Dragging her duvet to the wall. She sat on it, soft and padded after the worn, sparse carpet, pulling it around her shoulders, wrapping herself up in it.

And after all, it was probably nothing. Katrina didn't even like him. She said so herself. She was always making fun of him, talking behind his back. It was their joke. Hers and Katrina's. They'd laughed about him. They'd laughed about his stupid baggy trousers and the way they fell down all the time so you could see the top of his boxers. About the way he took himself so seriously, his boasting and his arrogance. They'd laughed about him. Katrina must be wanting her to hear, she thought. It was going to be their joke.

Tomorrow morning, it would be their little joke.

Something banged, hard, against the wall. Lucy jumped. Waited. Silence. Katrina's bed was by the wall. Katrina had put it there, dragging it from under the window on that first day she'd moved in. Lucy pictured the bed, Katrina on the bed, sitting up, leaning over him, her skin, she could almost feel it. She wanted to touch her on the shoulder. To make her look around and see.

There were noises now and voices, whispered urgently. She couldn't hear the words, but she could hear the tone of them. Then something that sounded like a table being dragged around, or was it the bed? She could almost feel it in her stomach, vibrating along the floorboards. Footsteps, then his laugh again, but less laugh-like now. It sounded unsure, scared almost, and Katrina wasn't laughing back, she was sure of it. He spoke. He said 'Kat?' It was a question, loud, urgent. He was saying other things too, his voice lowered now, deep, hushed, like the bass line from a CD being played one flat above you with the rest of the notes obscured by the distances between and just the lowest slowest vibrations transmitting through plaster and wood and brick. He spoke. He said, 'Kat'. It was not a question.

Lucy didn't call her Kat. Lucy called her Katrina, but maybe she preferred Kat, she didn't know. Tomorrow she would call her Kat, when it was shared, when it was their little joke, as it would be, she thought, would it be?

Something knocked against the wall, something soft, not bone, a palm, a hand, a foot. She tried to work out which end of the bed was where, breathing heavily. She was listening to the middle, she thought, yes, the head of the bed was behind her, the foot in front. It had been a foot then, stamping against the wall.

Lucy wanted Katrina to speak. Wanted to hear her words, to get inside her head, to know what she said to other people when she thought Lucy wasn't listening. She wished Katrina would speak but she didn't. *He* spoke again. It wasn't a word, it was a note, another bass note, like a cello bowed carelessly with too much pressure, the string creaking under the weight of it. Then Katrina spoke, a violin note, pure, singing, teasing, it had letters to it, it said No. Lucy loved it. The cello note was back, a repeated pedal note, an open string, pleading, insistent, slurred, tied, each beat accented, but then it stopped being a note and became a groan and she could hear it so clearly. He spoke. He said, 'Kat', and there was begging in his voice and Lucy hated it.

And now she could see him there, in her mind, tried to slash the image away, but it wouldn't go. She had to look, his body, naked, the image twisting in her head. She wanted it gone, but at the same time she had to know, to listen, to hear Katrina speak.

But Katrina was silent.

Then Lucy had the terrible thought that perhaps Katrina wasn't silent. Perhaps she was saying things, making noises, but they were for him only and she wasn't sharing, she was whispering in his ear and Lucy would never know what Katrina said. But Steve wanted Lucy to hear him. His groans were deep, boastful, like his laugh. Lucy pulled her legs in closer, hugging them to her chest, rocking, trying to think of Katrina but now she was thinking of him, of them, together. And with every groan sent to her through the wall she wanted him to suffer, to cry, to hurt, scream, bleed.

But then Katrina laughed. It was slow; an intimate laugh. But joyful too. Lucy hadn't heard her laugh like that before.

Lucy put her hand against the wall. Her palm was flat, open. Just one more sound. She stroked the wall. One more sound, just for me this time. Laugh again, because *I* want you too. Lucy held her breath. Silence.

She would wait.

Stonewall

Susan Kemp

A still leuk magneeficent fae a distance.

Yont whaur the fir trees brek, bauldy biggit upon craig, o rock, bensell-shapet see'd for miles aroon. I heard the guidwife say tae her man, afore they cam ower close, 'Magnificent!' She sain the samin wird thris. 'Splendid!' quo she. Then, 'Marvellous!' Ilkane braith wi a birr...

...Acht, dinna listen tae the Keep will you. Naebody kens what it's on aboot onyway an' it's no as if I havnae spent the last two hunert an' fifty-eight years teaching it tae onnerstan proper English. I've given up noo, I just try tae ignore it and you'd be wise tae dae the same.

Ane kin see ma kythe of force; a simboll of hardely won battels fought upon less skweemish times. Ma granit hairt rememberis weill the bluid and chaddy-guts o' lang deid kemps an hears yet aw the screams o' mittled Inglis prisoners...

...Haud yer wheest noo an' let me introduce myself. I'm North Wing, added to the central tower, The Keep, of Redheuch Castle by the Laird of Kiltully Glen in 1749 and paid for by the fidelity o' his son tae the King. His only son. His deid son. A life wis worth a wing back then if luck wis oan your side...

...Aw lang sin syne but nou thae twa, Guidwife an Man, maun draw near bedeen an tak tent of aw they unco things A canna turn a deefie tae nae mair: the ashlars an machicolations are rouned like bou-backèd old men an ma walls greet wi the stains o this hunert years gutterspill.

biggit – built; **bensell-shapet** - strongly shaped; **samin** –similar; **ilkane** - each one; **braith** –breath; **birr** - force, energy, enthusiasm; **kythe** - show, display; **chaddy-guts** - the large intestine; **kemps** - warriors of mighty stature and great strength; **mittled** - mutilated, tortured; **bedeen** - at once, soon; **tak tent** - observe, take note; **ashlars** - squared blocks of smooth stone trimmed to shape; **machicolations** - projecting gallery on brackets outside of castle or towers;

Why are you fretting aboot whit they two have tae say aboot the price of fish? Have you gone and changed your mind on me ye ramshackle pile of mossy rock? A 'splendid' here and a 'magnificent' there and you'd let me fa' prey tae any old passin' stone robber if they offered tae sandblast your parapet – is that how it is?

Dinnae be daft. This pair wid need wailth an stupit eneuch tae heave siller an the fires if they mynt tae get me sortit.

Aye. Mebbe if there were sons' lives left tae barter wi' you'd ston a better chance but for a' that I doot there'd be wealth enough, even in Royal coffers, tae dae a' that's needed.

We are nobil ayont the imaginaciouin of these hudderie-dudderie herrie-hawks. We'll stay so.

It's me that's the problem if truth be told. The Keep wid be a noble ruin lang aifter I returned to the sod even without all they laws, by-laws and in-laws. It's me who wisnae built tae withston' cattle carcasses being catapulted up ma enceinte. I was tae charm visitors fae London wi' my tall, glass windaes and elegant marble mantelshelves all set aboot wi' gold and precious china.

I wis a wallpapered aspiration, meant tae bring a breath of southern sophistication tae a boggy land. Mebbe if onybody had thocht to see if the credentials of the Laird's cousin's wife's brother who designed me added up tae much I might have been worth it yet, but it turns oot they amounted tae nothin at a'. In Forfar I might dae fine but on this craggy pinnacle wi' weather comin' in fae a' sides I need the constant graft of an army of servants just tae stay stonnin'.

The lady is aboot tae enter wi' a hard hat set strangely on her hair-do an' a glowin' orange jaiket glinting even in the weak sunlight. I am, officially, a hazard and there are warning signs strung aboot on every hangable surface fae the start o' the drive a' the way up, through, an' intae the back . I dinna ken why thy didnae just string a skull and crossbones fae the flagpole and hae done wi' it.

Gentie an denty North Wing stuid for ane hunert an fifty twalmonth, nae juist an aff-set. Thaur wis mirding, lauchin and many a daunce inside they bonnie walls. A hae hardtell anaw that at the time it wasnae til folk were short

---

siller – money; **hudderie-dudderie** – slovenly, dirty, tawdry; **herrie-hawks** – plunderers; **enceinte**, the enclosure or fortified area of a castle); **aff-set** – ornament; mirding – dallying;

soumed the dwyne of it begoud, as quikly as if Fate had awakit sudden fae doverin tae find Time nipping her heels.

Aye. Bit by bit just wasnae enough fir butler, housekeeper, maids, handymen, baker, candlestick maker. Not with work aplenty in the towns with fun tae be had an' money tae be spent. It followed then that we gave the rest o' the Kiltully family to the First War. In dribs and drabs. None returned. I remember well the third cousin, twice removed, who then came up fae London an' looked us o'er – just the once – before hurrying back tae the sanity of her Victorian Terrace an' putting us up for sale. I was glad she went away.

We stayed like that for twenty seven years, abandoned tae the tender mercies of the climate. I froze an' cracked, froze an' cracked. The pipes spilled water intae every corner in spring and I began tae rot fae my foondations up an' my gentle, polite yellow sandstone soaked in the excess like a deep water sponge. The Keep froze but didnae crack because they wa's of granite are two feet thick and the windaes nae mair than slits.

The third cousin eventually gave us tae some nuns for free and they lived in Keep and grew vegetables in my ballroom. They joined up at the end of 1944 and never came back either.

Since then we've been pushed and pulled intae a' sorts to suit whitever folk micht take a fancy tae living in a castle. There's even a swimming pool in Keep's dungeon that wis never used except by rats an' they maistly drooned. Noo I've damp mould burstin' through the flock paper covering ma wa's and on a windy night I could faw doon yet.

They plan tae dismantle me, this wifie and her man. They're going tae pull oot ma ivy an' take the less sodden hand-cut stones to sell one by one. Reclamation they call it. Do-gooding interference I call it. They dinnae gi' two hoots for the owls in ma crevices nor a monkey nut for the red squirrels in ma overgrowth and the hen harriers roosting in ma holey roof. They can get tae. The Keep and me have made alternative arrangements.

I have stuid for naurhand sieven hunnert years and wid stand yit anither sieven but fir the menseless cairy-on of donsie, shilpit men. I want oucht fir nocht fae these ignorant body keinds.

---

short-soumed – underpaid; dwyne – decline; begoud – began; **dovering** – dozing; **menseless** - meaningless; **donsie** - unfortunate, hapless; **shilpit** – puny; **body keinds** - human beings.

We'll be a bing of auncient aislarwerk and grunmale, buriet aneath the brach-an dern, hame tae aw the beasties, an when folk maun leeve a hameart way agin thay'll glagger fir the likes o us.

An' we'll aye be beautiful stone, carved by the hons of maisters. Oor age exposed. A story in fallen stone. We'll fa' here, where we were meant.

Go on then, Keep. Might as well just dae it.

Wi aw the history of ma stanes I gaither aw ma virr an shudder. The tap lum stairts a wabble but steidies ower swith – the airt of skeeled dorbies lang syne bygane yit tae the fore in ma design (the din wid fear the best of us an A see'd houndis in spede that'd be ahint the hatted pair as they run lik reiv-ers on a herryin). A draw doun intae the sowls o thas whase bluiwis skailt athin ma walls an shudder ance mair. Nou the lum faws in a bonnie airch. It taks a parpen wi it an twa windows aff North Wing. Anither stane faws, then anither. The hindermaist fae the entrance lintel condingly carvit wi forgotten wirds:

IN FIDELITAS

A wis built tae be the hame o kemps. Nae mair an nae less.

---

aislarwerk - masonry constructed of hewn stone; **grunmale** -rubbish consisting of earth and stones. **dern** - hidden; hameart - plain and simple; **glagger** - desire eagerly; **virr** - vigour; lum – chimney; **dorbies** - stone masons; **ahint** – behind; **rievers**– cattle thief; **skailt** - spilled, shed; **parpen** - a stone which passes through the entire thickness of a wall; **condingly** – lovingly

Hitch

William Gault Bonar

Dropped on the edge of some town, late, gettin colder. I should bed down, but I give it five. The second car stops. I open the passenger door.

'Where you headin?'

'Winnipeg.'

'Put your pack in the trunk.'

The interior light is dim. The driver's in his early thirties, neat haircut, tame moustache, tie loosened, throat exposed. No the usual type that offers a lift.

'C'mon, man, you drew the Winnipeg ticket!'

All the way, fuck it. 'Sure,' I say.

The car pulls out onto the road.

'You Irish?' he asks.

'Naw, but you're close. I'm a Scot.'

'Sorry, man. I shoulda known that.'

'It's a common confusion, no problem.'

The driver strains to speak over his shoulder. 'What you guys say your names were?' he says.

Someone says, 'We didn't.'

I start. There's two kids in the back, sixteen or seventeen. 'Hi,' I say. The boy nods.

'D'ya want some?' the driver says to me.

'What?'

He points at the bottle jammed between his thighs. It's already a good bit down. He seems all right, but maybe he just handles it well. We're well out of town now an I've heard too many bear stories to like the idea of gettin out here.

'Naw, I'm cool, man,' I say.

He shrugs, takes a belt, screws the cap back. Black mountains mass on either side. The big car strokes the highway, the black top contours.

'Y'married?' he asks.

'Naw.'

'Gotta girlfriend?'

'Maybe, back in Scotland, I dunno.'

'Right, friend, y'never know.'

The car takes a long curve, murmurin. I picked up a letter in Vancouver frae Bianca. It had the usual stuff: her sister, her waster father an how he treats her mother, her pals and truly borin stuff about work an this guy David gets mentioned.

'I've gotta wife.' The driver takes another pull on the bottle. 'I work hard, y'know? Got the apartment, all the stuff. I love her, man. Y'know whatta mean? Yeah you know, I can tell.'

A big moon clears a ridge. I watch the road. What am I botherin mysel about anyway? Davy boy is probably doin me a favour.

'Y'know your girl long?' he asks.

'Since final year at school. Y'know, high school. Five-six years. We've been livin together the last three years. It's not like it used to be, y'know?'

'Ain't it the truth, man? They get this fuckin itch. Got to make big eyes at some other fucker. And then they blame you. Say they feel trapped, that you're possessive, you're always criticisin, you're boring for chrissakes. Am I boring to you? Okay, I'm just an ordinary guy but I'm funny, man. People like me. Here, have some of this.'

'Naw, you're all right. Maybe later. I'm not big on alcohol.'

'You got some weed? C'mon, I told you I ain't boring.'

'I don't carry it when I'm travellin. The pigs like to pull over when they see you hitchin.'

'What about you guys,' he calls to the kids, 'you got some weed?'

I look over my shoulder and try silently to tell the boy to say, 'No.'

'We're out,' he says.

'What kinda fuckin hippies are you anyways?' the driver says.

But he's no angry, just windin us up.

Sometimes I watch Bianca wae other blokes in the pub or at parties. She tosses her thick blond hair that goes all the way doun tae her arse. She knows they want her. When she catches me watchin her, she has to say somethin aboot it that everybody can hear. 'Can you no find somedae tae talk tae? I'm no gonnae go in the bedroom wae him.' An she'll laugh an flash her eyes at the bloke. I grin like it's all a big joke; like it's all part of how we turn each other on an it's this bloke who's the patsy. But I get this big ball in my throat an twistin cords in my stomach. I get sick wae it. Sick that she makes me hate her so much.

'She likes this guy in the apartment building,' says the driver.

'Who?'

'My fucking wife.'

'Yeah, right, she *likes* this guy.'

'No, I mean she likes this guy.'

I glance at the kids. The girl is leanin intae the boy, her head on his chest, her eyes wide. The boy looks back at me an jerks his head taewards the driver.

'That's heavy. Are you sure?' I say.

'I'm fuckin sure, man.'

The car crosses the mid-line. I will it back.

'I just meant sometimes we get things wrong, y'know, read things in,' I say.

'I fuckin caught her. Today, I get home early and she's out. I go downstairs to his apartment, man. I get on my knees and listen. I can hear the bitch, y'know whatta mean? That fuckin noise they make?'

The left-hander goes on an on. I lean to the right, ridin sidecar. Bianca makes a lotta noise, deep in her throat, she sorta gravels. She never yelps or squeals or moans, just this gravellin 'ohh' that gets longer an louder. That first time I went down on her, she was so sweet. As I kissed and licked her she kept sayin 'naw' an 'what're ye doin?' An efterwards she clung tae me, shy with her face buried in my neck, though she wouldnae kiss me, said she didnae like the taste.

Now we hardly get started when she's pushin my head doun there an wrigglin up the bed. When she's had enough, she puts the heel of her hand on my forehead an thrusts me away. Never a word, never a fuckin word. But most of the time now it's just, 'Coorie in an keep me warm. Stop that wrigglin stuff.

Can that thing no curl up an go tae sleep?'

'It could've been somebody else,' I say. 'I'm not sayin it was, just that it might've been.'

'You think I don't know the sound my own wife makes?'

'Of course you do. I'm just sayin, through a door like that, with maybe another door in-between. Sound gets distorted, y'know. It's possible you heard somebody else, that's all.'

'Listen, pal. I heard what I heard. I heard my own wife fuckin with another guy. Do you think I get off on sayin that?' He's lookin hard at me now an the car begins tae drift.

'It's okay, man. I believe you. Who else would know if it wasn't you?' I nod at the windscreen tryin tae redirect his attention back tae the road.

'Look out, man!' It's the boy shoutin an the driver reacts, haulin the car back as it starts tae crunch verge gravel.

'What? You wanna drive the fuckin car, the driver shouts. You a fuckin wise guy? You wanna see some drivin?' He rams the gas pedal tae the floor and the big car takes off, fishtailin.

'He's just a kid,' I say, tryin tae keep my voice calm. 'He got a bit scared because I was upsettin you and I made you take your eye off the road. You're a great fuckin driver, man.'

But he's starin ahead now, both arms straight out, open palms rammed hard against the steerin wheel, fingers flexin as if they're countin up the acceleration.

'You've proved your point, man,' I say. 'We could run into a cop patrol. They'd take you in for this. It isn't worth it. She's just takin the piss, she'd love it if you were out of the way.'

'Oh yeah, you got a better suggestion?' he says.

I take a deep breath, anxious no tae lose him again.

'Damn right. Forget her. Move on. There's better things for a guy to be doin. You don't see me hangin around some chick who's takin the piss.'

'You wouldn't kill the bitch and her fuckin lover boy?'

'Hell, I'd like to. Any man would. But you've got to think of yourself.'

'You wouldn't kick that door down and go in with a kitchen knife? You wouldn't rip his fuckin head off? C'mon man, tell me you wouldn't strangle her with your bare hands.'

The car straightens out on a downhill an there's a moose, twice the size of a Clydesdale, tae the right o the mid-line, side-on.

I begin tae climb backwards oot o my seat. A coupla tons o animal will come through the windscreen an why no, why fuckin no? The girl makes a sound. The car twitches left an the road ahead is clear. Naebody speaks. The kids are wrapped around each other.

'Fuck her,' the driver says, 'fuckin bitch.'

Faith

Mary Paulson-Ellis

It happened like this. I was standing in church next to my Mum and we were singing. God's triumph is Man's redeemer. Or something like that. I'd sung one verse and was half way through verse two before I realised something was wrong. It was a kind of tingle in the air.

I looked to my left and right but everyone around me was just singing like normal, looking down at their hymn books, or up towards the ceiling. Then I realised. It was that I couldn't hear.

First the deeper voices had gone, then the women's sopranos, now even my Mum's had disappeared. Soon everyone in the whole place just seemed to be mouthing like a shoal of hungry fish, while the only thing I could make out was my own voice, kind of light and thin like it has always been, and a little out of tune.

I honestly thought I was going deaf. I turned to Mum and was about to put my hand on her arm when suddenly there was this other sound in my head. And it was the most beautiful sound I'd ever heard. I'm not exaggerating. It was like a golden liquid pouring into my ear.

I turned around, of course, and she was standing there, her eyes all shiny, gazing straight at me, singing and smiling at the same time. I turned quickly back and tried to concentrate on the page in front, but it was no use. Though she wasn't anything to look at, I knew straight away. It was as if I had been struck by lightning. On a Sunday too.

After the service I searched for her, but she was gone and I understood. These things are not allowed – miracles or divine intervention or being visited by the Hand of God. They tell us that they do happen, of course, but they don't mean to us. They mean to other people in other countries – people who don't worship in churches built next to main roads and newsagents like ours.

I told Mum I couldn't stay behind to help with the tea and coffee because I wasn't feeling well. Instead I went straight home and upstairs to my room to see if I could somehow catch my breath. But it was hard. All over my body, my skin seemed to be singing.

Then, a few days later, I saw her in the street. She was walking along as though nothing had happened. I followed her for a bit, trailing the tiny snatches of song that seemed to trickle after her as she progressed. You would never have believed she was anything out of the ordinary. Her shoes were such a normal kind of brown.

Eventually she turned into a busy road and I lost her, but not before she looked right at me and I saw how the sunlight caressed her hair. Then my afternoon took on a totally different hue. I went home and looked at myself in the mirror. Outside I seemed normal. Inside it felt as though time had stood still.

It's hard sometimes, to work out what to believe in. I've done a lot of thinking about this recently, but none of it seems to make anything clearer, or more distinct. Instead it seems to get harder and more confused. More like a jungle.

I believe in eating well and taking exercise and trying to keep an open mind. I believe in being optimistic – glass half-full rather than half-empty kind of thing – and in telling the truth as much as you can.

There are other things I believe in, even though I ought not. That if you walk under a ladder, bad things will happen for example, falls and trips and lost life savings, things like that. I know in my heart of hearts it's old-fashioned thinking, but I worry that if I don't throw the salt or stop the mirror from breaking other people will get caught up in a bad experience that ought to be mine – hit on the head by a falling brick perhaps, or sacked from work, that kind of thing. So I always avoid cracks in pavements, white cats, magpies and walking underneath anything.

I also believe in ironing, and polishing shoes, and in doing your best. That is very important, whether it is cleaning the dishes, or mopping the floor.

Of course, I believe in God too.

The next day she actually came to the door. Dad called to me from the bottom of the stairs. I came down expecting Monica and instead it was her. I hadn't even thought to change or brush my hair.

We went out for a walk. All the time she talked I could hear music playing in my ears. As well as her eyes and her hair I realised her teeth were shiny too and her skin had a kind of a glow. I wondered if I touched it whether my fingers would go right through, but it was her who touched me first, gently, on the arm, to gather my attention. I can still feel the spot where her thumb pressed against my cardigan.

She asked me lots of questions. What did I like doing? Who were my friends? What was my favourite thing?

Do you believe in God? That was the first question I ever asked her. She looked at me funny before she laughed, little chimes dancing about her in the air. Then she kissed me.

Afterwards she answered, I don't know.

I do believe in hell. Not the burny, burny kind, but the never-ending torment kind. I mean I can see it in life right now, everyday life I mean. Look at the faces of people going to work and back when it's pouring down, when the train never comes and never comes. Things like that. And especially when they get older – the older the more miserable, with their trolley bags and folded up newspapers, trudging, trudging, trudging. I can't bear it.

Then there are the women who end up married to the wrong men, and the men who end up married to the wrong women. I hear them sometimes in other people's houses, through the walls and even in the street. Everyone says, whatever happens, that these people are stuck together forever.

And after all, nobody's perfect. Even my Mum with her Hail Mary's and early morning visits to the Mass. Even she's in trouble. I saw her with the man we call Uncle Steve. The way she patted at her hair when he came to visit for tea. So hell, I do believe in that.

In the end she left, of course. She had to return to her own town, to pick up the rest of her life. That is what she told me. She'd only been here on holiday. Part of me was relieved.

But whatever I do I can't shake her now. Every moment we spent together seems to be held in a different part of me. The soles of my feet remember the time we walked on wet grass. My spine carries the imprint of her bedroom wall. Once we took a bus to the countryside and climbed a hill. It was her suggestion. She told me jokes all the way up, and stories all the way down. Now every time I breathe, laughter and Once Upon A Time's curl inside my chest. My heart, of course, that doesn't know where to begin.

I've tried to think of what else could describe it, but I only ever come back to this: when they put that wafer on my tongue, my eyes half closed and everything we had been taught swimming in my brain. I know I felt it then – him, God, whatever – because it has stayed with me ever since and I've always found it easy to believe. It's just that no-one told me she would feel the same.

Though I have not said, they understand that something has gone wrong. My Dad frowns now when I am around. Mum pats my arm and says, Not to worry. Pray more. But it doesn't make me feel any better. I even thought of telling the priest, but when I started he just said, Uh, huh, as though it were a matter of opinion. Well, how do you go on after that?

I still go to church and sing, of course, even though I do it now for different reasons. I stand and I open my mouth and sound comes out. I look up at the ceiling and down at my hymn book. But all the time, all I am feeling is her breath tickling the soft part of my neck, under my hair.

And there are certain things that I don't believe in any more. About men and about women and about love. Because when you are struck by lightning, well, you can't ignore it. We all have our secrets, even from God. This one is mine.

Origami

Kirsty Logan

Another paper cut. Rebecca's hands were a mess: swollen with tiny cuts, peppered with dry patches. She'd have to make sure they were all healed before Sean got home, or he would know what she'd been doing.

She checked the clock. Almost six: she'd better get some dinner on. She pottered around the flat, checking the front door was locked and deciding which soup to heat.

Sean was supposed to phone tonight. It had been nearly a week, but the phones on the oil rig were always in high demand. Rebecca understood, even though it was a shame that they had such little phone time. At least Sean only did trips of a month: some of the engineers were away for six months at a time. Men with wives, children, pets, and friends they didn't see for half a year. No wonder there was a mad rush at phone time. The men must be so lonely, stuck in the middle of the sea with no-one to love. Weeks of meals for one, falling asleep in front of the TV, watching happy couples in bars and shops and restaurants. Stuck in the middle of the city with no one to–

She was halfway across the living room carpet. She must have been wandering towards the TV, or maybe the bathroom. The cupboard was that way too, but she wasn't about to make that mistake again.

She hurried over to the cooker and took the soup off the heat, the inside of the pan crusted with blackened chunks. The smell of burning filled her throat.

At five to eight Rebecca was on the couch trying not to stare at the phone. The pan, bowl and spoon were washed and drying by the sink; the TV was tuned to a reality show. She was fiddling with the pages of the TV guide, but only because she was nervous about Sean's phone call. The pages were forming into fingers. With her thumbnail, she scored lines of knuckles on the paper fingers. She placed them carefully on the coffee table, then started folding some toes. The paper was thin and brightly coloured, the knuckles folded across faces and times.

She resisted the urge to pick up the phone on the first ring. She carefully arranged the paper digits, then answered on the fourth ring.

'Hello?' She tried to sound husky, like she was halfway through a cigarette.

'Hey, Becks.'

'Sean, baby.' She bit her lip: that was too much. 'How are you? How's work going?'

In the silence, she heard her muffled words back through the receiver.

'It's good. Busy. Look, Becks, I've only got a couple of minutes.' He paused, but she didn't say anything. The delay meant that they'd only end up talking over one another. 'I'm really sorry, but they want me to stay on for another week. I wouldn't, you know, but we could use the money.' Rebecca listened to the clicking quiet after his words. 'Becks? You there?'

'Yes! Yes, I'm here. Sorry, the delay. I thought you weren't finished.'

'So it's okay? About the extra week?'

Rebecca swallowed the lump in her throat as she stared at the cupboard door. 'Of course. You're right, the money would be nice. But you know –' she coughed 'I'll miss you. It's lonely here without–'

'Becks, you won't–' They both started talking at the same time, and had to spend a few seconds saying: no, you go.

'Becks, it's just that ... I know it's stupid, but last time ... I mean, that ... you wouldn't, right? It's stupid to ask, but I worry about it...'

Rebecca's cheeks were blazing. Even though Sean couldn't see her, she did her best innocent smile.

'Of course not. Don't worry, love.'

'I know. I'm sorry, I shouldn't have asked. Anyway, that's my time up so I'd better go. I'll call the day after tomorrow, same time. And Becks?'

'Yes?'

'I really miss you.'

'I miss you too. Bye, Sean.'

Rebecca hung up the phone. She collected the paper fingers and toes and walked to the cupboard door. She closed her eyes, held her breath, and opened the door.

Later, halfway to sleep, she was pleased that she'd managed to throw the fingers inside without looking. Looking would lead to touching, which would lead to bringing him out of the cupboard, which would mean he'd be in this bed right now. But it was just her, so she'd won. She wasn't lonely, she was victorious.

Rebecca woke from origami dreams, familiar shapes folding into strange forms. Eyes still sleep-glued, she ran her hands through her hair, feeling something hard and rough against her forehead.

Clenched in her palm was a crumpled paper hand.

Her whole body jerked. She threw the paper hand across the room, watched it bounce off the wall. It lay silently unfolding on the carpet. She lifted the duvet, scanning the warm darkness for foreign body parts. There was nothing but her own pale legs.

When her heart had slowed to a normal pace, Rebecca got up. She dressed without looking at the hand.

By the end of the day, Rebecca was exhausted. Avoiding paper might be feasible for a builder, or a sculptor, or a bartender; for a legal secretary it was impossible.

Much of her work was done on computer, so she'd thought she could manage; but she'd forgotten about the memos, post-its and phone messages that snowed onto her desk throughout the day. By mid-morning, her waste-paper bin was full of crumpled body parts.

But working hours weren't the only problem. During her lunch break, she paused mid-sandwich to fold intestines from her newspaper. Walking out of the office, her nervous fingers made an ear out of the tissue in her pocket – luckily the thin sheets wouldn't hold the shape, and unfurled as she threw it on the pavement. On the journey home, her bus ticket became a tongue.

When the bus reached her stop, she tore up the tongue and stuffed it down the seat. She kept her fists clenched as she walked home.

Rebecca was watching the news with her hands held between the sofa cushions. She'd tried to clear all the paper out of the house, but there was just so much of it: newspapers, novels, receipts, wrappers, bills, magazines. Different colours, weights, textures, patterns. Magazine pages were eyeballs: colourful, and held a shape well. Broadsheets were limbs: large enough for a whole leg. The TV guide had already become a pair of kidneys, and it wasn't safe to let her hands roam any more.

Rebecca jumped when the phone rang, but she sat still until the fourth ring.

'Hello?'

'Becky, hi. How are you?'

'Yeah, you know. Keeping busy.'

'Good. I'm sorry I couldn't call earlier. I queued for the phones every night, but it's so busy. I had to give up or I'd have missed my sleep.'

'That's okay. You'll be home soon, and then we can talk any time we want.'

Rebecca listened to her muffled echo in the receiver, then the crackling quiet. She opened her mouth to speak.

'Becks, about that. They offered me another week. You know you were unhappy with me missing New Year, and with the new shift pattern I'll be home right into the start of January. So it's better really, right? Becks? Rebecca?'

Rebecca stepped back from the cupboard door. She was already at the full reach of the phone cord; to open the cupboard, she'd have to put down the phone.

'I'm here, Sean. And it's fine. I'm glad you'll be here for New Year.'

'God, Becks, I'm so glad. You're not feeling...'

Lonely, thought Rebecca. Lonely lonely lonely.

'No, not at all. I'm actually going out with Jen tonight, so don't worry. I miss you. But I'm keeping busy.'

'I miss you too. I put your photo beside my bed so I see you last thing at night and first thing in the morning. Your photo isn't very chatty though. I miss saying good morning and hearing you say it back. But look, I have to go, the phone queues are huge tonight and everyone's giving me the evil eye.'

'Okay. I love you.'

'Love you too.'

Rebecca waited for the dial tone, then placed the phone at her feet. She smoothed down her skirt, neatened her hair, and opened the cupboard door.

The man inside had paper hands, paper legs, paper lungs. He had eyeballs, toenails, a paper heart. He was missing some bits – spleen, eyebrows, a left heel – but that didn't matter.

Rebecca helped him out of the cupboard, arranging him carefully on the couch. She flipped to the channel she knew he liked, and settled down beneath his arm. She nuzzled his cheek and stroked his broad, creased chest.

He was incomplete, fragile, imperfect. But tonight, she wouldn't sleep alone.

The wittol

Tom Rae

Aw Jesus, the knurls wur shuiting up!

As if testing a marrow for over-ripeness, Rob's fingertips massaged his skull gently, probing tender spots under the wounds where healing bone still ridged like uneven ice layerings on the millpond. Compulsively inserting forefingers into the deepest furrows he traced lines to where they grew. *Christ, aye, the scurs wur boukit.*

Then, as they did every morning, the crusted scars began to itch and the throbbing started.

Aw Christ, Aw Christ! If only his hair was long again … but the surgeons had shaved his cantle and it would take another ten months at least before Reid Rab Borthwick had his wild red locks again. But if the knules grew like this for another week he must find a bigger bonnet. He needed to see what they looked like.

Sweat runnels tickled him, damp linen creased annoyingly under him, the dawn chatter scraiched at him, until the room slowly grew light enough to rise from the bed, wipe himself down, and pull some clothes on. Last of all Rob fitted the tattered green bonnet he'd been wearing since Beltane. Folk would be asking again today why he should be wearing a cap this muggy July.

Rob crept across the corridor, remembering the creaky board in the doorway as he slinked into Anne's room. Anne and the bairn's room now; when he returned from Flodden before Yule his wounds had been too painful to share a bed with his wife.

To get to the mirror he would have to pass the crib. Anne was asleep. But hidden from him by the sides of the cot, he could hear the bairn's delighted wee cooings and gurglings. The boy was awake and if distracted would he squawk?

Rob tiptoed across to the mirror, suddenly appalled when a tiny hand shot up over the side of the cot. The forefinger and pinky pointed at the oak beams, the middle fingers clenched shut. One of the midwives said they might never open.

Soon he was past the cot and in front of the mirror. Glancing back at Anne he could tell she was in deep sleep because her lips puckered open and shut in steady puffs. Sleep brought an innocence to the face that reminded him again of the girl she had once been. Or was it the way the fair curls stuck to her forehead as she turned from the damp pillow?

Rob peeled off the velvet cloak with which Anne superstitiously covered the mirror each night, and stared at his tired face. It wasn't just his wounds and the pain. Even before they marched south last Michaelmas he'd been feeling every one of his two score years. That damp autumn he'd felt shame when he shirked from putting his full weight behind the shoulder that heaved the guns through mud. That was work for the young loons. But the know-how of Maister Gunner Reid Rab Borthwick, and four hundred oussen, had brought James his cannon just in time.

Maybe it was just this mirror. That was it. He wasn't so old. His father lived well past sixty. He'd just never before seen himself in such a fine looking-glass. Compared with their old one it was like palming the frost from the surface of a frozen pond and suddenly seeing your face in clear grey ice. They could never have afforded this mirror, a gift from the Comte d'Aussi for billeting himself and forty Frenchmen on the farm. Little use the French pike training did the poor Scots lads. D'Aussi explained that the mirror was glass painted with mercury and tin the Venetian way, and insisted they take it, a small token. Venetian guns were the best too.

Eyes tight shut, Rob clasped his hands over the bonnet, felt the sharpness probing his palms, but resisted the urge of fingers to explore. The surgeon warned him the bones of his skull might never fuse, but the jagged ridges would at least be hidden when his hair grew. Now the ridges were forming crags, and even before he closed his eyes tight and pulled off the cap, Rob suddenly knew what he would see in the glass when he opened them.

His right horn protruded further than the left, was almost as big as an ivory dagger hilt; only, unlike a dirk handle its shape was the same delicate crescent, its colour the same yellow sheen as a new harvest moon. The left kippie curved crookedly towards the right, misshapen spurs of bone at its base dirty with dried blood. Behind him the bairn clawed at his rattle and giggled...

...was still clawing and giggling as Rob closed the heavy scullery door behind him and headed across the pasture, remembering as he entered the Bell Wood that he had forgotten to cover the mirror with Anne's cloak.

Patches of sunlight on the woodland floor thinned as he made his way deeper into its shade. Here there were no whispers, no smirking sniggers, no resentful widow glances that he should return quick when their husbands did not. Here he could remember painfully his blouster about the size of his big guns, what they would do to English ranks under his aim.

The Dog Days were bearable here, and if he found a refuge of rock, or fallen tree he could hide and wait for dark with clenched fists and eyes shut tight and the screams inside his head denying the agonies scouring at his skull. Here he could forget the chopping pikes and the hot gun barrel roasting his broken leg.

He didn't need to look where he was going. These were the woods of his boyhood, the woods where he had courted Anne before they married, the woods where they'd come years later to see Aggy the wise woman despite what the priest would say if he found out. The woods where they swallowed Aggy's foul brews, repeated mocking incantations and lay together in pools of damp moonlight. Remedy was none.

And today Annie wouldn't miss him. Would be well rid of his embarrassing presence about the farm. It was his own fault.

He had encouraged them.

At first he had convinced himself it was a miracle. He should have died at Flodden and God had decided to leave them an unsired son. But Rob lived. And God wouldn't be lied to. He slumped. God wouldn't be lied to.

'I thocht ye wur a deer, Rab.'

Rob looked up.

Aggy Maciver, a basket of mushrooms underarm smiled staring at his bonnet.

She kenned, the auld bitch kenned their secret.

'How's Annie? And the bairn?'

'The wee wan's fine. The wife's moody.'

'Ach Rab, weemin ur lik that. Fickle as the moon's horns. Whut'll the bairn be noo then, three months?'

Aggy was stooping to pick some scuttling thing from the undergrowth as she spoke, rolling it gently between dirty fingers before secreting it in the pocket of her smock.

'And fit aboot thon French sodjer loon? Did he get killed tae Rab?'

'Ah cannae remember.'

This was true. He forgot things now. Or the words wouldn't come. His head ached.

'That's a shame. You and Anne were richt fond o the French loon? He wiz aewiz up at the farm, eh no? Here Rab, tak this.'

Aggy handed him something hard and wet from the apron pocket.

'Dinnae look at it now. And dinna chew it. Jist swallow it. That's it. It'll help yer heid. Looks like we'll be having rain for St Swithin's Day efter aw Rab,' said Aggy, as he ignored the wriggling hardness in his mouth, and swallowed.

When he wakened he knew from the Church bells he'd slept for hours. The scouring in his head had stopped. Instinctively, Rob reached for his wound as he rose. The horns were still there.

He didn't mind.

As he reached the edge of the wood, he snatched off his bonnet and threw it into some bushes. He didn't need it. He could thole this.

Rob reached the chapel just as the deacon was closing the heavy doors. He edged past him with a nod, didn't notice the turning heads and stares as he limped down the aisle towards his family. Anne turned, wee Rab cooried in the crook of her arm. The wean reached up and grabbed at a coat toggle with his peedie claw hand as Rob stroked and marvelled at the silky darkness of the boy's head.

As Rob sat beside his wife she reached up and caressed his broken cantle. She smiled. Someone coughed.

It was Father Kennedy, patiently waiting to start Sunday mass. All eyes on him now, he began:

'This day we will consider the words of the prophet Jeremiah. Chapter 3: verse 3:

Therefore the showers have been withholden, and there hath been no latter rain, and thou hadst a whore's forehead, thou refusedst to be ashamed.'

Slight catch

Kate Tough

I step off the bus and stand where I landed; no part of me ready to go home. I watch the bus continue on into the distance; start to pick up speed, stop to let someone off, start, stop. All that curbed potential.

My mind searches for things I could do at this time on a week night.

Sensing it might take a while, I move inside the bus shelter and perch on the sloping, plastic pole that passes for a bench. A woman in joggy bottoms walks by: supermarket bag on one arm and yoga mat rolled up under the other. That's one way to spend your evening. But is it a life: a job, a hobby and dinner at nine o' clock at night?

Maybe I'll look through my phone, see if there's anyone without children or an early start who might want to meet me for coffee. Much less relaxed than I was before I went out this evening, but the theatre wasn't the problem. It was being on my own when I wasn't in the mood to be.

As I scroll through searching for a companion, the thought of holding another conversation suddenly wears me out. I've spent the last couple of months out in public, yakking, or home alone, silent. What I really miss is being quiet in the company of another. I need to be quiet. I don't need to be alone. Nor do I need to foist this on anyone else at this time of night. I put the phone away and stare up the street.

A short, shabby man teeters towards the bus stop, hand resting on the open can nestled in his pocket. Not judging distance too well, he sits down right next to me so our upper arms are touching through the bulk of our coats. I wait for his uninvited, incoherent ramble. The half-cut, half-arsed attempt at conversation he will make and I will be expected to invest myself in, in case he causes a scene or stabs me or something. Conversation that he will apologise for starting, 'Sorry, hen, sorry to bother ye,' but will proceed with regardless.

Conversation that will quickly move into the realms of the personal, 'Yer a lovely lassie. So y'ur. Where's yer husband tonight, hen?' And I will have to shout my answers, because he's drunk and deaf, so passers by will hear me say, 'I'M NOT MARRIED,' and he will reply, 'Lovely lassie like you? Courtin then, aye? Boyfriend, then.' 'I DON'T HAVE A BOYFRIEND EITHER.' 'Och. That's no right. Come oot wi' me, hen...' Does he honestly think? 'See when ah wiz younger? Quite a looker. So ah wiz. Ah'll take you oot, hen. Aye. Up the dancin...' At which point he will get up and step from side to side, turn in methodical circles with his arms out, all the while smiling and carrying a pretty decent melody of a sixties song. And I will sneak off to leave him to it.

But this is not what happens. Our upper bodies rest beside each other and I can smell his sour skin and breath but because he doesn't say a word, doesn't even look at me, I don't feel the need to shuffle along. We sit in contemplative silence. When I contemplate what he might be contemplating I realise I have no idea and start to like him for this. What are the thoughts of a chronic alcoholic? I'm filling with respect for his choice to step out of the coherent world into his own world unfathomable by anyone else.

He sees a bus approaching and reels to his feet. I presume he wants to get on it so I stand and stick out my arm on his behalf. As it slows towards us I hand him my day pass to use for his fare, then resume my position on the bench. But I don't want to sit here any more so I start heading down the street thinking I'll walk off some of this antsiness and then maybe I'll be able to go through my front door.

If I were in the mood for a steak pie in a tin or a dust-covered notebook, I'd be sorted because there's a jingly-bell-on-entering newsagents every 20 yards but not much else is open – except a couple of pubs where I'd be a whole day's drinking behind the regular clientèle. Approaching the next junction I see large panes of light just beyond it... an Internet café. That'll do. Cup of something and an email check. Pushing the door with the level of force it looks like it needs it flies away from me, the handle bouncing hard off the wall. All eyes on me. Bloody cardboard door.

Usually when I log on to Wahoo I'm not exactly rushing, but I'm not far off; email being a necessary inconvenience in the day. Tonight, however, time is like the 40 pots of yoghurt you need to get through to claim the picnic rug. No immediate need to click on 'mail'. Instead I glance over the Wahoo home page. There are celebrity stories and links to proper news, to the weather, horoscopes, health, even dating. A quick look over each shoulder and I click.

The link goes to a dating site whose name I recognise from the telly. Am I actually about to do this – click 'enter'? How anonymous is it? Can the café trace which sites I've been on? I remind myself it's not porn – but being caught looking at porn would be slightly less humiliating.

I glance behind me again then click.

Navigating the Catch.com homepage, I struggle to compute this new, abundant reality. The last time I was in the market, occasional successes depended on a blend of kismet, alcohol and making the effort (to get out the door, to look half decent). Now, apparently, it's as easy as doing your weekly shop on-line – in your raggy pyjamas with your hair unwashed if you like.

I type in my 'preferred location'. When I go to select an age range I swither. My gut says 33 to 43. But what if my perfect partner is 32 and I never meet him? It's only a playful first search. Anyway, I know I want to meet a man, not a boy, so 33 to 43 it is. Pages and hundreds of men appear – available, interested men. No guesswork (is he single? Will he come over and talk to me?) just get-on-with-it. Bizarre. The thing my single friends were always telling me was impossible to obtain and might never visit one's life (AAAAHHHH! As scary as the tales of other things that might: cancer... marriage...) is now on tap. No more waiting and wondering. Here is an arena where single people can take the initiative and guarantee themselves a date and in all probability, a relationship. It's too much. I log off. The world I'm living in is not the world I thought it was.

Too late in the day for coffee, I order tea at the counter. I carry it towards the tables, noticing the content of a PC screen as I pass; someone else is looking on Catch.com. High from the hitherto unknown world I just ran in and out of like a kid on a dare, I take the table offering the best view of this guy's screen. Watch and learn. He scrolls down a long page of profiles. Sometimes he clicks to open one up – must be when the photo is a winner. From what I can make out, the women he's looking at are about my age. He looks about 40; slim build, expensive, up-to-date denims and muddled hair. What's the world coming to when a guy like that can't get a date by normal means; when single

people stare at screens in search of what's sitting right next to them? I foresee
the movie that ends with us getting married. The breakfast TV interview:

'Yes, we met while we were internet dating – separately, on computers that
were side by side.'

'How adorable!'

'I know! Isn't it?!'

Should I brass-neck it and approach him? 'Excuse me, I couldn't help noticing what site you're looking at.' Then what? I can't. I'm not bold enough.
But when I think of walking out without saying anything I see days of self-
recrimination ahead. He's on a dating site, after all, he's hardly going to be
offended by an approach. I rip a page from the back of my diary and write:

> Forgive my intrusion, but I noticed you
> were surfing Catch.com. Me too.
> What are the chances..?
>   name – Jill
>   age – 34
>   location – here
>   employed – yes
>   kids – no
>   email – jb_70@wayhay.com

Disembodied by nerves, I fold the note over, put on my coat and step
closer. He's tapping away on the keyboard, giving me my first glimpse of his
left hand and the ring on his third finger.

A nice vanity

Amy Burns

The house was build from stone. Underneath 65 years of paint and wallpaper the walls were tongue and groove. The windows worked on rope pulleys and the hand-blown window panes were thick. All the rooms were finished with wide, honey-coloured, curly-maple baseboards. Ben and I pretended to know things about foundations, helical piers, shower pans and shingles. The real estate agent pointed out a niche worked into the stone fireplace. *A great spot for a cuckoo clock,* she said. I decided that was what I wanted, a house with arched doorways, glass doorknobs, hardwood floors, butcher-block counter tops and a special place to put a cuckoo clock. Ben's parents paid and we moved in.

Late at night we sat outside and listened to our neighbour's wind chimes and thought we should get wind chimes too. Many nights Ben would ask, *Do you want to get high?* But I didn't want to get high any more and so we just sat in the shadows beyond the orange security light or we'd lie in the hammock together. We were newly married and newly aware of a sleepy suspicion that left us both quiet and sure of nothing.

When we were married almost a year, Ben decided that he needed hobbies. He bought all the things he needed to make his own beer and took guitar lessons. I naturalised our yard with a bulb sampler from the nursery: hyacinths, crocuses, tulips, daffodils. I also learned to smile at our neighbours while they handed out advice for mulching the azaleas and pruning the plum tree. I planted two sugar maples in our front yard because I love to watch sugar maples turn in the fall. The first year they were planted, I gathered a basketful of dark red leaves and I kept them in the house until they were crisp enough to shatter against a whisper. Ben joined an independent soccer league that practised three times a week and played away games every other Saturday.

Just after he started playing soccer, Ben decided it was time to start a family. He wanted to have children while we were still young. The first time I thought I was pregnant, I started collecting baby names in a fabric-covered book. The last time I thought I was pregnant, I came home from the doctor's office and pulled up the linoleum in the kitchen. I found more hardwood floors and I used mineral spirits to clean them. Ben decided to go back to school.

He enrolled in geology classes at the community college. His teacher was Joe Spindle. Joe was much older than Ben but didn't look like it or act like it and he said he didn't feel like it. Joe started coming to our house, having dinner, getting too drunk to drive home, spending nights on our couch. On those nights, Ben always wanted to have sex with the bedroom door open. He pushed me against furniture and always wanted me to turn my back to him. He asked me one of those rough nights, as he pushed my face against the cool dresser mirror, *What do you think about throwing somebody else into the mix? Wouldn't matter if it was a girl or a boy whatever you're comfortable with.* I didn't answer but I cried while he finished fucking me and when he was done I went into the kitchen and got an orange out of the refrigerator, stood in front of the sink and peeled it. While I was eating the orange, Joe turned on the television. I looked in the den, Joe was looking back. It was 3 am I didn't say anything, just turned and went to bed. Ben was already snoring. The room smelled like sweat and bourbon.

I started working at a florist that was five blocks away from our house. On the way there I passed the church where we got married. The sidewalks in front of the church were buckled and cracked from the roots of two old oaks. I wondered how I didn't trip as we ran out on our wedding day, as I threw my bouquet, caught birdseed in my hair and down the scooped neckline of my beaded dress.

I worked at the florist for five months putting the green in funeral stands, sticking leaves into dense, wet oases that soaked overnight in water and fixative. Ben decided to get back to nature. He and Joe hiked the bluffs a couple of miles outside of town. They took regular, overnight trips to see caves in different counties. Not long after the trips began, Joe made a habit of talking directly to me. He asked me what I wanted to do with my life. He asked me if I regretted getting married so young. He told me that he worried about me because I seemed to have such a pasteurised curiosity for life. He said we should get to know each other better. He said nice things about the sugar maples.

The afternoon I quit the florist, I walked over to the elementary school. It was summer and the parking lot was empty. I found two pink barrettes which I put in my pocket. I walked to the edge of the school yard, to where the public school property stops and the Lutheran church property begins, to where the Women's German Heritage Club planted pink fairy rose bushes that clung to the chain length fence and made it almost pretty. I pinched off a rose hip and looked through the fence at the house where the Governor used to live.

By the time the breeze started blowing cool again and the leaves on my sugar maples started hinting at something other than green, Ben said that he'd never felt more alive. He celebrated by getting a tattoo of a whale on his calf. 'Tlingit,' he said. I put two coats of water seal on the basement walls to keep everything from moulding.

I mowed the grass for the last time before the weather got cold. Ben and Joe pulled into the driveway with two new mountain bikes in the back of Ben's truck. I was sitting on the porch steps drinking water. Ben pulled himself up on the railing so he wouldn't have to walk around me. Joe walked up the steps beside me and moved past with a touch.

Their conversation was easy and immediate. They talked about plans for the weekend, chicken pox, spirituality, a new thing Ben found that was great for blisters. Joe talked about his ex-wife and his child. I stopped listening. I was daydreaming about a retainer wall that I wanted to set into the hill at the front of our yard, skirting the sidewalk. I could plant things that would trail away and look like they had been there for a long time.

I went inside to take a bath. As I soaked in the hot water, I could smell a bar of glycerine soap lying on the porcelain edge of the tub. I closed my eyes.

When I heard the bathroom door open, I said, *I'm in here.*

Joe said, *I know.*

Shut the door!

I grabbed a towel from the floor and wrapped it around my body as I stood up. I could feel the air from the hallway deflected by the heat rising from my reddened skin. Hot water soaked the towel.

Where's Ben?

Joe laughed. He leaned over and put his hands on the old piece of furniture I'd refinished especially for the bathroom. I'd cut a hole in the top for the sink and holes in the back for plumbing. Joe said, *This makes a nice vanity.*

I drive by the stone cottage every time I am in town, even though that's not often any more. I haven't lived there for a long time. Ben's painted the shutters navy blue and started building a privacy fence but has never finished it. The last time I went by I noticed children's toys in the yard and a car I didn't recognise parked next to Ben's truck. Somebody has built a new mailbox, trying to match the stonework of the house. It's time for a new roof, too. There's been some storm damage. My sugar maples are still there though, getting fuller and softly shading the front yard just like I knew they would.

Bookends

Alison Sommerville

He told her every week that she was beautiful. She thinks this is because he never really saw her from the place that he saw herself. He was a writer. She was tired of words and wanted to think in pictures for a while. She was in the mood for travel. Everything had been so involved lately, so serious, always negotiating where he's at, where she's at, where the relationship is going. She felt the need to disentangle herself from their fiction, to remove herself from his story.

She decided to change direction, south to London where there would be none of the haphazard meetings and small town coincidences that plagued her in Glasgow. His friends always wanted to know how He was, what He was working on. Her friends read his books like detective novels eager for clues about their relationship. Helen and Simon, the talk of the town. Once she had accused him of plagiarising her life. He told her it was art, fiction, that she had nothing to do with it.

'You,' he had said, 'could see yourself on a postage stamp.'

She needed to be away.

The bus trip is like a slide show. Windows, frames, motion. Headphoned and happy she sleeps and wakes at irregular intervals and is glad of the empty seat beside her.

The back streets of Covent Garden lead her to a market stall where they take photos of people dressed up in old-fashioned clothes. She remembers when she and Simon went to the coast. They asked a passing tourist to take a picture of them with their faces pressed through a wooden caricature of

Mr. and Mrs. Penguin. Simon uses the photo as a bookmark. They look like a cartoon. She decides to go into the stall. The idea intrigues her. Faces on the wall smile down at her, eyes wink in encouragement, a gentleman presses his moustache into his face with his thumb and first finger, contemplating her appearance no doubt. She is the stranger here, surrounded by pictures of the past. All shapes and sizes in sepia tones.

There is a smooth-skinned mannequin in the corner. Helen circles it. The arms are poised as if in dance. A fan hangs lifeless from the wrist, the string lodged in the crack of the join where forearm meets hand. On the third time around Helen is close enough to feel the ostrich feather hat against her cheek, her nose, her mouth. Soft whispers against silent lips. Her hand sweeps the length of the skirt, she rustles the taffeta between two decisive fingers.

'How much?' she asks the bored looking girl wearing a black T-shirt and red lips. 'How much for a photo?'

'Twenty quid,' says the girl, getting up from behind the desk, her face becoming slightly animated. 'You'd look great,' she says, attempting a sales pitch. 'Really, come into the cloakroom and we'll find you something to wear.'

They walk towards a red velvet curtain. Helen notices sleeves and toes sticking out here and there, is reminded of her mother's wardrobe where she would play for hours and hours, lost in a carnival of hats and coats. Helen smells the same musty smells, clothes crowd in all around her, lace and pearls are taking her back...

She is interrupted by the girl sliding garments across the rack. The screech of steel on steel.

'Here's one,' says the girl, happy to have found something. 'This ought to do.'

She scans the dress at arm's length. It is red and black checked with a black frill. Somehow Helen had imagined something softer, prettier.

'Hold out your arms,' orders the girl.

She threads Helen's stiff arms into the rolled up sleeves, her blue cardigan bunches at the elbow. Then she occupies herself round the back with pins in order to get a good fit. Helen stands still and feels an array of pins and tucks, tugs and tensions. She is longing for cloth on skin. The girl smells of pepper-mints and cigarettes as she fastens the buttons at the neck.

'There you go. Oh, almost forgot, the hat.' She reaches up to secure a pink feathered hat. 'Don't worry about the colour, they're all in black and white.'

Helen is hot. Her jeans feel cumbersome under the long skirt, her trainers out of place. She hears the rustle of the material and imagines the swish against naked ankles. She had wanted to linger, to slowly peel off her old everyday clothes and replace them with fine silks and satins. As she walks towards the camera she feels a stray pin sticking in her back.

She hears the whirr and click of the camera and rearranges her face into a smile. She sits stiff-backed and uncomfortable. A few people have gathered to watch, she sees them out of the corner of her eye. The girl hides behind the black cloth of the old-fashioned camera. She comes out to take the fan from the mannequin and place it in Helen's hand before returning for two more clicks. In a minute Helen is back in the changing room struggling with pins and buttons, trying to undo herself. The girl is back behind the desk reading a magazine. She knows that she will not pick up the photo even though she has paid her money.

Money. She needed the cash and the work was easy enough – just take off your clothes and sit still. She was used to it now, she even enjoyed it, sitting naked as they glanced and stared at the various parts of her body, translating her into timid brush strokes, strong curves, defined lines. She wondered about the nuances of her flesh. Did it show that she ate too much, slept too late, made love to two different men in the same week? How much of the inside could you see from the outside?

'In writing you read between the lines, in painting you read behind the lines,' she heard the tutor say in his softer than soft voice, sepia-toned.

Helen loved that voice, she would let it carry her around the room from easel to easel, student to student. Sometimes the tutor would linger long enough to take hold of the wrist of one of the students, sliding it into a long slow arc of movement like a dance step. She knew the students well enough now that she could sense their movements with her eyes closed. The boy with the glasses smudging her black to grey, softening and blending, combining light with dark to create the blur of a pubic triangle. The girl with the ponytail gave her nipples so red she was sure they were bleeding. She could keep still for a long time. She would float up and away from her body, outward and upwards into the spaces between the desks and people or she would find herself concentrated on the worn edge of a crayon.

Simon had not been too pleased about her modelling. He was still writing. Pink and yellow unlined pages stuffed into small white envelopes. They would arrive in the post, she would read them indifferently. She had read it all before. He was busy with his work, there was no room for her. No, she was not coming home yet. She was savouring the distance, exploring the tension, enjoying the space between them. Long, slow days without him. She could almost hear them tick.

The back streets of Charing Cross lead her to a bookshop A small bell rings as she opens the door. A boy sits behind glasses reading intently and chewing his bottom lip. Her feet are tired and crowded, she wants to take her shoes off and sink into the soft carpet. Mozart plays as she strolls the corridor of books. She runs her hand over the smooth straight spines and follows the line of the shelf with her eyes. The small bell rings again as someone else comes in. Annoyed at the interruption, she decides to leave. Outside she stops to have a look at the window display. She sees her own face reflected in the glass, frozen, shocked, distorted by its stillness. An image, her image, on the cover of a book, his book, one of the students, a drawing of herself is reflected back at her like a kaleidoscope. Multiple copies fill the display window. Surfaces are shifting beneath her. One of the books is turned the other way, on the back cover is a picture of him, smiling. Helen and Simon, the talk of the town. She turns and walks away, turns her face from the image, feels like she's been turned inside out, like she is the negative not the photograph. Feels each step as she turns and walks away from it all.

Flightless

Barry Gornell

She left. The last he ever saw of her was the heel of her red shoe. That and the ring she no longer valued. The ring he had slid onto her finger less than a year ago, that she had placed on the brown Formica table. His breathing slowed with his heart. He rose from the large armchair. His legs ached from having only sat on the edge of its horsehair seat. He looked across the table to where she had spent the night, facing him. The faded counterpane on the still made bed held her shape. He took his ring off. He tried to put it on top of hers exactly but it slipped. His lay against hers, barely touching yet together.

The room door clicked closed behind him. He put the hotel key on the desk at the bottom of the wooden staircase. Outside, the dry rectangular patch by the kerbside showed where their car had been. She had taken it, heading south. When he walked away to catch a train in the opposite direction the dry patch was gone and he was heavy with rain.

They both stood in the room and looked at the rings. He didn't know what to say. He wasn't sure why she'd brought him up here to see them. He thumbnailed dirt from beneath his fingernails, flicking the results on to the floor. He'd seen this before, had two cheap rings in his desk drawer in fact, amongst the paperclips and ballpoints, abandoned years earlier. These were gold, he could see that.

'Why don't you take them?'

He saw in the deep brown of her eyes that she was shocked by his suggestion.

'They look expensive,' he said.

They did. And yes she could do with the money and yes it would be nice to take somebody else's belongings to the pawn shop, especially items unwanted such as these.

'They might come back,' she said.

Disappointment ran through her voice like a headache in a hangover. This wasn't like her. She was usually his first smile of the day; often the only one.

'You reckon?'

'I hope. It's a sad place for it to end.'

He considered the room. There was no arguing with her judgement. It was a weary space, inspiring neither hope nor optimism. The dark-framed bed and the mossy green furniture combined with the ageing wall covering to give the impression of a forest glade that seldom felt sunshine. Stains on the ceiling, like the rings of a tree, confirmed frequent rainfall. Last night's stain was fresh and wide. The thunderstorm had filled his hotel for the first time in years. The thought crossed his mind that had the rain not been torrential the couple who had belonged to these rings might have continued on their way and bought morning coffees as steam rose from the road.

'Okay,' he said, 'let's wait and see.'

He knew he'd insulted her. He said nothing, fearful of making things worse.

Their relationship never recovered.

They returned to the formality of employer and employee and were conscious of the respect they showed each other in their dealings. Nonetheless, she was grateful for his not letting the room. In truth, the hotel was never full again. Progress connected the northern cities to the commerce of the central belt with a major roadway. It bypassed the small town and rendered his small hotel insignificant. Trade no longer passed.

They both had time on their hands.

She knew from the ghost of cigar smoke and the occasional forgotten tumbler, the whisky dried to a circle in the glass bottom, that he spent frequent evenings alone in the room.

She came to take pride in the dust that gathered over the rings while she kept the rest of the room spotless, though no less gloomy. They shone through like hope and belief; at the same time indistinct yet precious. To move them would be giving up. She would sit with them at the end of her working day, smoking cigarettes, drinking coffee, looking out the window as though their return was probable, never mind possible.

But you can only sit for so long.

When she did come back, the maid was long gone.

He felt like an old man.

The room was no longer cleaned weekly. The hotel was barely alive. He'd taken to sitting outside; trying to pretend it wasn't his. She climbed from the car, closed the door and leant back against it, her weight on one leg as she rubbed the back of her calf with the other black shod foot. She looked tired. She wiped her face, both hands palm flat, working away from her nose, stretching the loose skin across her cheekbones as though to banish years of fatigue with one gesture. Her fingers passed across her eyes, like curtains opening onto the past.

'Can I help you?' he said, even though she didn't look like a customer. Nobody did any more.

'No, just looking,' she said, pulling a loose-change smile from somewhere.

He regarded the flaked paint of the hotel's frontage, the faded curtains; the letter deficient sign.

'What at?'

'My biggest mistake.'

He leant forwards.

'How's that?'

'Took a wrong turn here, long time ago now.'

'How can one wrong turn bring you back?'

She almost laughed.

'Just keep driving.'

He knew it was her; that it was her ring that lay on the table in the room upstairs below the other. He knew that she had been the one to leave. Her being alone spoke of an unhappy return. Her voice was a husk of cigarettes and searching. He stood and walked across to where she had parked, not knowing that it was the same space from which she had once left. She watched as he prepared himself. Everything about him looked sidetracked.

He looked at her and she let him. She was handsome and probably no younger than him, but looked as though she was running out of courage.

'He's dead isn't he?' he said, his throat dry.

'He's gone, yes.'

She turned away.

'If you've nothing pressing,' he said, 'there's something I'd like to show you.'

He turned the key in the lock and pushed open the door. When she stepped inside she was where she had long wanted to be, only too late. Eighteen years of being wrong decanted. She stood in the clarity of that bygone day still wishing she could change it. She could smell rain. She could smell his after-shave, his vigour, his sweat as he argued for their future. She felt again the loose movement of her clothing on her body as she rose and kissed him, insisting it was for the best, sure she was right, convinced she was destined for better things, feeling sorry for him. She heard the blessing in his goodbye. She sat on the bed opposite the empty armchair.

Looking down at where she had left her ring she saw his.

But the ripe smell of cigar smoke wasn't his. It filled her nostrils, scented her tongue. She felt the warmth of the sun against her legs as it burned through the window. She realized that the bed wasn't made. It was stripped down to the mattress, faded blue and white stripes, lacking a couple of buttons. She wasn't there. She was here.

'You take a whisky?'

She nodded.

He poured a bumper and handed it to her. He poured one for himself. He was looking at her again. Her face was lined with her every regret, each line silvered with tears. She drank with two hands wrapped around the glass. She sniffed.

'Why didn't you move them?'

'She thought you'd come back.'

'Your wife?'

He smiled, grateful that she thought he could at any time have been married.

'The maid,' he said. 'She found them. She didn't want to move them.' He offered empty hands by way of an explanation.

'That's nice.' she said. 'She believed in love.'

'She believed that two rings couldn't be the end of the story.'

He drank deep and then placed his glass on the window sill, the remains levelling in the bottom of the glass.

'She got that right.'

'She did.'

Rising from the window seat he poured another glug into her glass. He put the bottle down within her reach, though not so close as to suggest she was obliged to drink any more.

'Why haven't you moved them?'

He scratched his cheek stubble with all four fingernails. The truth rippled up his back. His scalp tingled. The words tumbled out.

'Maybe if I left them, she would come back.'

He knew these were the right words. His loneliness exposed, he avoided her scrutiny. He chose instead to focus on the two rings. But he could only stand it so long. He made his way to the door. He turned back to her on the threshold.

'You have plans?'

'None to brag about.'

'You're welcome to stay.'

Doxy

Jénnifer Ádcock

'I'm not being any fun, am I?' My voice came out pathetic and weak. I wasn't trying to be melodramatic, I was pointing out a fact. But Sukh wasn't bothered either way. He was sipping his *agua fresca* like there was nothing wrong in the world. I couldn't understand him— I disappear and check myself into hospital without telling him, and he, instead of ditching me to enjoy his trip, goes to all that trouble to find me.

'Oh, don't worry about me. I had a nice long walk down Reforma and the most deliciously folkloric breakfast in a market stall. So cheap as well.' His sunglasses sat fashionably on his balding head, and his little finger stuck up as he answered his hi-tech mobile phone. It was her again.

'...well, she's smiling, and the doctor said she should be up and ready to go in a couple of hours.' Just from the way he spoke to her I could tell she was trying not to sound jealous. 'I'm gonna take her to Teotihuacan. She hasn't been there either, can you imagine? Living so near by... yes, I love you too, baby...'

Baby she was indeed — only 19, studying to be a doctor and waiting patiently for him to change his ways.

'How did you get here?'

'Taxi,' I managed.

'Did you have to walk long to find one?'

'Not really.'

'Must have been hard if you were in so much pain. You could have called me, you know.'

'Shut up.'

'Are you coming to Teotihuacan? And then we can have dinner in a nice restaurant. On me of course.'

I closed my eyes, sleepy on painkillers, and dreamt of her, injecting poison in my drip, saying something like, 'Sorry, dear, but it will be so much easier for all of us this way.' And me replying, 'Oh, I don't mind at all, as long as you two are happy. By the way, I love what you've done to your hair.'

When I woke up Sukh was still there, smiling the most irritating smile at me.

'Why are you here?'

'I was worried about you.'

'No, I mean, why are you here, in Mexico City with me, instead of in Chicago with your girlfriend? Don't you love her? Don't you mind hurting her?'

'I do love her, and I hate hurting her, but it's the principle of it. If we are going to be consummate, free individuals we need to follow through with what we want.'

'What are you talking about?'

The nurse came in to unplug me and told Sukh I was doing fine and was free to go to the pyramids if I wanted to, but I shouldn't eat spicy food or drink any alcohol.

'What about smoking?' asked Sukh.

'She should never be smoking, stitches or not! And remind her to take the pills the doctor recommended.'

Outside the hospital Sukh bought a huge charro hat and was determined to wear it for the rest of the trip. People in the subway were amused. Hey, *pinche chino!* they called out as I stumbled along, aching all over.

She rang him again when we were climbing the Sun pyramid. I was less interested in their conversation than I was in trying to understand how a bunch of people long ago could have spent their lives building these huge constructions that served no function whatsoever. How could all that effort have possibly made sense to anyone? Did they understand at all what they were doing? Did they do all this just to have people like us climbing it, thousands of years later, wondering what the point of it was? A man-made, civilised mountain, with stairs on it for us to climb all the way up to some ancient god. I suddenly remembered how much pain I was in, and sat down on a bit of stone. Sukh finished his phone call and came up to me, looking very concerned.

'You're not stopping here, are you? We need to get to the top! I thought you said you were feeling Okay enough for this. Are you Okay? We can go back now if you're not feeling well.'

'I'm fine, I just don't think I can climb any more. I'll sit here and wait. You can go, don't worry.'

'Well if you're okay then let's climb to the summit. It's a once in a lifetime opportunity!'

'I can come back to Teotihuacan some other time,' I said, stealing my cigarettes from his pocket. 'Now go away, I want to smoke and sit quietly for a while.'

I watched him climb up the steep, narrow steps. At one point he turned around and waved at me with a big grin on his face. I looked across to the pyramid of the Moon, and the avenue of the Dead, and some ruins I couldn't identify because I didn't bother reading the guide. I was amazed at the dimensions of it, at having just walked across that vast, yellow land, blotched with bushes and tiny colourful tourists. I had seen pictures of this in history textbooks, but couldn't grasp actually being there. What if when I was a kid, reading those textbooks, someone had told me that when I grew up I was going to be sitting half-way up the Sun pyramid, smoking a cigarette, being the other woman. Maybe I would have imagined lots of intrigue, and lots of shouting, like in the soap operas. But it was so much more boring than that.

Some teenagers asked me if I could take their picture, and they took mine. *Sonrisa colgate*, they told me, showing me my picture on the display. They wrote down my email and promised to send me the picture when they got home. And they did. I still have the picture, and like to look at it sometimes. Why I am smiling so eagerly in it I don't know. It had started to rain, I had stitches on my side, and I was hanging out with some idiot in a *charro* hat that kept talking on the phone with his girlfriend.

I remember that on our way back to the hotel, the taxi driver asked us, in English, where we were from. There was no hiding the fact we were tourists with him wearing that stupid hat. I kept quiet while Sukh very enthusiastically narrated the story of his life: born in Mongolia, grew up in France, now living in America, on a short trip to Mexico, etc. I watched the streets turning, the lights everywhere. The taxi driver explained that he didn't like America. He had lived there illegally and the law was too strict. Better in Mexico where you're free. As for France, he liked the way the government helps its people. He added, as a side note, that he was taking this winding shortcut through lots of alleys because he was trying to avoid the blockades from protesters. He must have noticed I was worried, not sure whether he was giving us this long, philosophical ride because he wanted to kidnap us or charge us extra money, or if he just had the habit of talking with his passengers trying to work out if they were dangerous. Sukh, thrilled about an opportunity to discuss politics, explained it was a crime to take hard-earned money from people who are doing well for themselves to give it to lazy poor people. Any government was corrupt by nature and had no place in trying to bring 'justice' to the world.

'France is on the path to ruin,' he concluded triumphantly.

'Well, you might be right,' said the taxi driver, 'but I still don't think it's right to have children begging in the street while the rich drive past in their big fancy cars.'

'Yes, but nature itself is cruel. Human beings' liberty is more important than—'

His phone rang again. I wanted to ask him to let me speak to her, and explain that I didn't want to steal her boyfriend. I had really only come on this trip with Sukh because I couldn't afford to travel here, and I didn't even get to do the things I wanted to do in Mexico City because I ended up going into hospital. But I didn't explain any of this. I was afraid it wouldn't come out right, or that she wouldn't believe me. There was probably nothing I could do that would ever make any difference for her. Or for Sukh, or myself, or even the taxi driver.

Cutout

Lucy West

It was Angela's second visit to London. She had been once with her mother, but that was before the war. As a child, she had been struck by the city's rush. Figures in overcoats and fashionable dresses had weaved through the bobbing masses as Angela gripped her mother's hand. Now, from her seat on an underground train, she saw a city covered in grime. Soot had laid its murky hand across every surface of the train and gently mottled every cheek with its grubby fingers. She looked around the faces of her fellow passengers. Most looked grey with the day's exhaustion. She thought of what was to come, and a shivering sweat wriggled through her body.

Angela stepped off the underground at South Kensington. She jostled among the evening crowds, climbed two sets of stairs and made her way to the exit. The station was bustling and a line of travellers stood swaying, lighting cigarettes and reading newspapers in queues to buy tickets.

She found herself in a sombre underpass plastered with adverts and filled with the sound of a violin. The tunnel wound round to the right and as Angela followed, she saw the source of the music: a dark-haired man of about 50, his face contorted in concentration. Angela noticed a change as she came into his line of vision: the furrow in his forehead relaxed, but he did not smile. Instead, he bowed slightly, closed his eyes and played the piece more furiously than before.

She emerged from the underpass on to Exhibition Road at the precise moment that the evening darkened from blue to black. Leaves circled around her, lunging and rising in the autumn breeze before settling in heaps upon the ground.

Angela had contrived a way of walking which felt rather unnatural, and betrayed her conscious effort to stay calm. Her stride was uneven and clumsy, despite her attempts to affect poise. She crossed the road and lingered outside the Victoria and Albert. She had only meant to stay for a moment but her eyes could not help but follow the wooden grain of the building's enormous doors. Her pupils darted from left to right as she tried to memorise every detail of the seemingly impenetrable entrance. The repeating pattern of the doors began to haze and a lamppost nearby illuminated a sepia kaleidoscope. The blurry nonsense of the door clicked sharply into focus and she raised her eyes to the men carved in stone above. Their faces glared as the breeze picked up a little, making branches quiver along the roadside. The central face bore a sharp look of disapproval and, just as the features morphed into a terrifying clarity, Angela's mouth became dry and sour. There was a buzzing sound inside her, her stomach lurched and she began to swivel on her heels. Stumbling towards a bench, she drooped against its wooden frame.

She cast her eyes down as a man and woman passed. They linked arms and whispered to one another, but did not approach. Angela's eyes misted and she blinked back stinging tears, concealing her face with a silver compact mirror while blindly pretending to fix her make-up.

The pocket of her coat burned with the guilt of its contents, but Angela felt the slump of dejection. The uncertainty of what was to come was too much. Thoughts of hiding, of running, streamed through her mind, but the memory of her promise was haunting. She stood up unsteadily, smoothing her coat and dress, and took a moment to recount the route that she had memorised. The branches of night-blackened oak trees arched above her as she continued along Cromwell Road.

Three figures came into focus: a couple and a little boy. The man rested a hand on the shoulder of the child, who was swooping and guiding a small model aeroplane through the air as he walked. The woman spoke in a relentless staccato chatter, but the man said nothing. He smoothed his hair with his hand and nodded to Angela as they passed. She looked away and walked with a little more pace.

The church was a white stone building with steps leading up to two large doors. Reaching the top step, Angela pushed the door. It did not move. For a moment she felt relieved. It was locked. At that moment, the door opened and a small elderly woman wearing a black mantilla stepped out. She looked at Angela, muttered something in French and held the door behind her. Angela paused for a moment and decided to turn back. There was no shame in leaving now. She stood aside as the old woman gave off a sigh and shuffled down the stairs. Angela placed a hand in her pocket. She was oblivious to the contents of the tiny packet that rested between her finger and thumb. There was no doubt that she was curious, but it was best not to look – that's what she had been told. Deciding that the worst would soon be over, she swallowed her indecision with an audible gulp and pushed the church door open.

The church glowed with a muted solemnity. Huge marble pillars held up an intricately painted heaven of saints and angels. Four people knelt in the main body of pews, their backs hunched in solitary prayer, their faces covered by hands. Angela genuflected uncertainly and took position on a kneeler at the back of the church, in front of the shrine to St Patrick. Flanking the altar were a stone war memorial and a confessional box. A square of light glowed from the box and it spread across the floor as the curtain was pulled back and a young man stepped out. Never averting his gaze from the floor, he knelt down directly behind Angela as she buried her head and pretended to pray. She held her body stiffly and obediently, sure that she would feel something. She could hear the young man's whispered meditations but he spoke with such a fast and breathy voice that she could only make out the refrain of: 'May God forgive me.'

Angela closed her eyes. The whispered prayers had stopped. Her heart was ready to leap forth from her chest as she knew the moment was upon her. She felt nothing.

She took the sounds of anxious breathing from behind as a cue to rise to her feet and walk towards the empty confessional. Sitting on a wooden chair padded by a scarlet cushion, she was separated from the priest by a gilded grille so that she could see only the shape of his hawkish nose. She pulled the curtain over, saying, 'Bless me father, for I have sinned,' then murmured every one of her secrets through the grille to the priest in a low, sad voice. The shadow of his head nodded slowly against the wall in response to her quiet confession. When she had finished, the priest paused, gave her a penance and asked her to reflect carefully on the consequences of what she had done.

Kneeling again by the altar, there was no sign of the young man. The few remaining worshippers were now leaving the church, each of them dipping a hand into the font by the door and making the sign of the cross with a small bow. Angela closed her eyes and pressed her face into the crook of her arm. She mouthed the words of her final Hail Mary as she blinked one solitary tear. Her task complete, she breathed deeply, blessed herself and made for the door. She too dipped her hand into the water in the font and there on the ground behind it lay a small, leather suitcase, just as they had planned. She looked from left to right and made as if to fix her shoe. Then grasping at the handle of the bag, she slipped out of the door into the darkness of Brompton Road.

She put her hand into her pocket. The package was gone, as she knew it would be. She expected her pocket to be empty, but there was something there. It was a small, white envelope with an A scrawled across the front. Angela's hand trembled as she fingered the lip of the envelope. With one movement, she ripped it open and pulled out the letter. The short, smudged handwriting was familiar. The letter read simply: 'I'm sorry. I have to go'.

Behind the wheel

Jessica Parkinson

I'm packing. Shirts, socks, underwear. My good shoes are still caked with mud from when we went down to the ravine after semi-formal. I sling them on top. It feels like June was years ago. I throw a look over my shoulder, my hand on the light switch. I wonder if I should clean up or something, put my sheets in the laundry basket at least, but I don't have time.

The Late Show's on TV. I can hear Jay Leno's voice booming from the family room where Dad passed out an hour ago. He'd finished the rye. The empty bottle was sitting on the coffee table last time I looked. The Coke ran out this afternoon. He told me to go down to the corner store for him, but I didn't feel like it. He said, 'You're a useless pile of shit.'

I said, 'Did you go to work today?'

He was wearing his terry cloth robe and he had a heavy five o'clock shadow. He had the heat jacked up so he could walk around in his bare feet like he was on the beach. I went to my room and opened the window. I didn't think he'd drink the rye straight. How should I have known mom had called this morning? Maybe she thought I was at school, but she didn't ask to speak to me. I usually get up for *Price is Right*, about eleven.

We'd both been home all day, but he didn't say anything about the call until he stumbled in a few hours ago, picked up a t-ball trophy from when I was about six, and sank down on the end of my bed. I shifted my legs over. He ran his finger along the contours of the bronze figurine and wiped the dust off on my sheets.

'There's a movie starting on City TV. Gonna watch it?' he said. I kept my eyes on the screen where I was leading Mario to the Princess for the millionth time.

'Nope.'

'I'm sorry, all right?' he said.

'All right.' I hoped he wasn't going to start snotting and whimpering like he did last time he came to talk to me like this. That hunk of junk t-ball trophy could easily set him off about how it was when I was young, about the family.

'Us guys got to stick together, right?' he said.

But he put the trophy down. Then he told me about mom calling. My thumb went kind of limp for a second, then I stopped listening and pushed down hard on the controller. Mario jumped on a magic mushroom and gained the power to shoot fireballs out his mouth. Chris thinks its lame how I still play the first Mario Brothers. But it's the best one. It's not challenging any more, usually just relaxing.

I consider taking the Nintendo, but somehow that seems like a kid thing to do. I turn the light out and pull the door closed. I slip along the hall past the family room. Dad's keys are on the silver tray by the door. Mom put the tray there so she'd stop leaving her keys in weird places, and then freaking out and being late for work. Her garden shoes are still sitting in the hall, like she might come back and do some weeding. They're about a century old, but she brings them out every spring and puts them away again in the fall. I stand there with my hand on the doorknob listening to Jay doing his interview, but I don't really hear it. The house is super quiet. Then Jay tells a joke and the audience explodes on cue with laughter. I go out and close the door behind me.

I'm glad I'm wearing my winter jacket. It's November and it dropped below zero a couple of nights ago. It's only going to get colder now. I work the front door key off the ring, separating the double circle with my thumb nail. I crouch down and listen for applause before I take a chance and mail it back through.

The car's parked on the street. He still does that out of habit. Its hood's plastered with old leaves from the poplars and maples. I walk over to where the front end is rammed against the curb, the front tire bent into the cement. The driver's side isn't locked. We don't get break-ins on our street. I slide behind the wheel and dump my bag on to the passenger seat. I'm not used to it being empty. If I'd sat my test a year earlier, I would have missed graduated licensing. But I've always had either mom or dad driving with me. They didn't like it any more than I did. I had to remind them I'd never pass my test if I couldn't practise. They were still talking to each other then, and they'd barter, negotiate their way out of it. Dad saying he'd do the dishes or whatever, if mom would take me driving, that kind of thing.

I put the key in the ignition and check the gear shift's in neutral. Chris said I was crazy learning to drive manual. I fiddle with the rear-view mirror until I can see the street behind me. I can see Chris's house three down from ours, but he's not there. Chris is a year older. He's in residence at Guelph University. I should have fast-tracked and got out of high school early. I should have seen this coming. I check the glove box for a map. Ontario's been folded into rectangles so many times the seams are ripped through. I chuck it on top of my bag for later. The lights are still on in our bungalow, but I'm pretty sure Dad hasn't woken up. I push the clutch down and shift into reverse. My feet work like a teeter-totter on the clutch and accelerator. I try to keep them even but the car stalls before I move an inch.

I slam the wheel with my palm. Dad'll probably report me. The car's just a small piece of the pie, my piece, I've decided. They can play rock-paper-scissors for the rest of it, or whatever they're going to do. I shift back into neutral to turn the car on again. I put it in reverse, ease the clutch, press the accelerator, and jerk backwards. There's a thud. The back wheel jumps over something and lands back down. I hit the brake and the car stalls again. 'Shit.' I grip the wheel and look hard into the rear-view as if there'll be a clue in there.

I don't want to know. I don't want to have killed someone's puppy or anything. I just want to drive away. My hands start shaking. The wheel feels really cold. I run my hand over my face and realise I'm snotting just like dad. I grab the handle and kick the door open. I squat down and see the lump under it. It must have run out from the Lawson's yard, because its nose is pointing at the middle of the road, towards me.

I've never seen a fox so close. I had a Robin Hood stuffed toy fox from the Disney remake when I was little. That's what flits through my head when I see him. A fox wearing a green dress. But he looks wild, like something I shouldn't be able to see. There's a dark patch on the tarmac. It's his blood, seeping out of him. That's his life all fucked up. I lay down in the road and just look at him. His eyes are closed. The fur on his head is almost glowing, more dark orange than red. I'm so close I can see the individual strands moving in the air that's trapped under the car. I get a weird feeling like it's really sad not to have that stupid Robin Hood fox any more. It's probably in the back of my cupboard. They'll throw out all my junk and bargain for the other stuff in the house. They won't bargain for me though. This morning they decided I'm old enough to choose for myself.

I can't help it, I know he probably has fleas, but I reach out to touch him. My fingers feel the velvet fuzz on his snout, as the last spark in him flares. His head flips up, his mouth opens and snaps. I yank my hand away and hit it hard on the tarmac. His yellow eye has popped open.

'Fuck you too,' I say. But I know it's because he's suffering. My hand hurts but he didn't get his teeth in. I get back in the car and start it up again. I don't stall this time as I reverse the front wheel over the fox. Then I shift into first, rev the engine, and drive over the body again.

Not black and white

Joyce Henderson

Shona took another sip of her tea and wondered what was on Jack's mind. What had prompted him to visit in the middle of exam week? They were both supposed to be revising. He could have picked up the phone. Then again, she knew Jack. If he had something important to say, he'd do it face-to-face. Maybe he'd guessed. Well she'd just bide her time, she wasn't going to make it easy for him. She curled up in the shabby leather chair, enjoying the circular living room lit up with May sunshine and the familiar scent of Jack's patchouli. His lanky frame made the two-seater sofa look like something from a doll's house. She wondered when he'd last changed his shirt. She'd teased him recently about wearing his favourite tartan one for a whole week, but he told her he'd had it on inside out for the first half. Jack cast his eye around the room as if he'd never seen it before and, nodding at the wall behind her, made his opening salvo.

'They Victorian builders must've called the architects all the bastards of the day for this one. Christ even the door's got a bevel on it!'

Shona turned her head to look at the door.

'Aye, but I don't think bevel's the right word for it, Jack,' she answered, turning back to consider him again. She knew he wasn't in the least bit interested in the shape of the room.

'Well you're the bloody builder's daughter, titch. What would your dad say about it?'

Jack had been about six foot since they were fourteen, but they had too much else in common for the height difference to come between them. He called her his bonny wee pal when he was drunk, titch when he was being himself, Shona when it was serious. That was how her countrymen were – a wee bit abusive in their affection. She was meant to understand that.

'He'd most likely call the architect a feckin eejit, just like your Victorian builders,' Shona said, faking a Belfast accent – badly.

'Except your dad's no Irish.'

'No, but the architect might've been. You know how my dad likes to speak the lingo.'

Jack made a huff sort of sound by puffing air out of his nose and looked away, trying to hide the slight smile at the corners of his mouth. You had to interpret these sounds, make the most of them. No Scottish man was ever going to throw his head back and guffaw at something a woman said, no matter how funny. She'd learned the names for each sound in her linguistics lessons: this one was a nasal plosive. No wonder she got on fine with her linguistics. She had an innate understanding, handed down by generations of discouraged female ancestors.

'Shona are you seeing another guy?' Jack uncrossed and recrossed his long skinny legs.

There he'd come out with it. What a relief.

'Aye... I am,' Shona admitted.

'It's that black guy I see you around the university with, isn't it? Genesis-Exodus or whatever his bloody name is,' Jack was looking at her straight in the eye now. Shona returned his gaze.

'It's Ezekiel, Jack. All the African guys have biblical names – their mums wanted to please the Jesuit teachers.'

'Humph.'

(That was aspiration followed closely by a bilabial plosive.)

'Have you told Sam?' Jack wasn't letting her off the hook.

'No, I can't bring myself to tell him.'

She got up and switched the stereo on. She'd been playing a Joan Armatrading album over and over. There was a track on it she wanted Jack to hear – *The Weakness in Me* – the lyrics telling a story about a woman trying to choose between two men.

Shona met Sam in a basement jazz bar in Edinburgh's New Town at someone's twenty-first. The guy who'd invited her had disappeared as soon as they'd made an entrance. It turned out he had his eye on the birthday girl and just wanted to see her face when he arrived with someone else on his arm. Any woman would've done. So he'd plonked her down at a table with some of his medic friends, Sam among them. Sam asked her what she did. Suddenly studying for a general arts degree seemed utterly inadequate.

'I'm an apprentice poultice maker,' she told him. Sam gave her a serious look, took her in. But he wasn't finished.

'And where do you practise the dying art of poultice making, may I ask,' he pursued, leaning a bit closer towards her across the table. They were all listening for her answer.

'In a small shop in Leith, actually,' she said.

She knew her ignorance of the subject would soon be exposed but she couldn't stop herself, couldn't see a way out after starting with a lie.

'The best poultice I ever had was in a back street barbers in Venice,' he said, going on to talk at length about the hot towels saturated with fragrant unguents the barber had applied to his beard before trimming it.

She had been devoted to Sam ever since. Jack knew that. She'd spent her holidays with him in Northern Ireland just because she couldn't bear to be parted from him, despite the car bombs, the hunger strikes, the tanks in the street. Once, during a rugby match that Sam was playing in, the only girlfriend on the sidelines, she'd got bored and wandered off out of the park. She found herself in the sights of a British Army rifle. The soldier was on manoeuvres, only needing someone to focus on as he crouched down practising for the real thing. It was nothing personal. Surely, being there with Sam was beyond the call of duty. She loved her man. She planned to marry him and have a sweet baby boy who looked just like him. Her mum and dad had opened a special wedding savings account at the Bradford and Bingley.

A friend introduced her to Ezekiel one lunchtime in the refectory. Of course he didn't have a look in. But it didn't put him off for one moment. He pursued her for months, following her around the corridors of the university, waiting for her in the café at lunchtime, even trailing her back to the flat. He was so brazen one time he came up the close and knocked at the door when Sam was there. She hadn't been flattered by all this attention. He was really too 'other', with his strange vowel sounds, his cocoa-coloured skin and his African features. She didn't want to be racist but it was hard sometimes to follow through with your politics into your personal life. Anyway, she was devoted to Sam. Sometimes he phoned her at the flat and, if Sam was with her, she would pretend it was someone else from her course or say, *sorry, wrong number*. Just like the Joan Armatrading song.

One Saturday, she and Sam had a conversation about what would happen when she graduated two years before him. She would have to go where the jobs were – take Norman Tebbit's advice and *get on her bike*. There was nothing in Scotland for arts graduates. If she ended up in London, would they stay together? That was what she wanted to know.

'It just isn't possible to predict that, Shona,' he said, citing how long it would take him to qualify and the precariousness of his financial position till then.

They were standing in the kitchen, sheets and towels trailing just above their heads from the pulley, her flatmate's dinner cooking in the pressure cooker – everything in together, meat, potatoes, cabbage and coming out in double-quick time tasting of nothing. The valve gave off a high-frequency hiss that altered the acoustics in the room and threatened to drive you insane. She could see the queue for the Odeon snaking around the square. Local Hero was on.

'I think you need me too much, Shona,' Sam continued, kissing the top of her head in a conciliatory sort of way.

When he'd gone, she fetched her toothbrush from the bathroom and a clean pair of knickers off the pulley and, putting them in her handbag, set off across the square, along Buccleuch Street and into the Meadows. She hesitated for a microsecond before she knocked on the door.

Ezekiel answered with a bag of clothes pegs in his hand. He showed her into his bedsit, offering her the swivel chair in the middle of the room, while he finished hanging out his washing. When he came back, he knelt down in front of her, one hand on either side, holding onto the armrests. He leant back to make some room and spun her around – once, twice, three times – before bringing the chair to a complete stop in front of him. He parted his lips, which reminded her all of a sudden of the flesh of a peeled plum, and he leant in.

The distance between us

Maria Di Mario

Do you remember our first kiss? It was after three weeks of flirtation, at a party on Woodlands Drive. We sat on the floor of a dark hallway, the taste of whiskey and red wine mingling in our mouths. Your hands through my hair, on my neck, my hands on your face, your unshaven chin scratching me, kneeling as if praying in the dim light, with sore knees from the thin carpet. After a while we went on to a party that was happening at your flat. We looked at the stars as we walked through winter streets to Barrington Drive, where we kissed on your bed for hours. When I put on my coat you asked for my number, and when I stepped into the street the sun was shining.

Do you remember the first time we had sex? Hot skin against skin, hot hands, mouths, faces, bodies pressed together, urgency made us clumsy. You ripped the button on my skirt. My shaking fingers struggled with your shirt. You accidentally elbowed me in the head, we laughed a lot. And then, oh, your skin against mine, and your hands, eyes locked to mine, hot kisses, feeling you against my insides. Your wide hands on my narrow back, your voice in my ear saying you wanted to crush me into you, so that our skin and flesh and bones and organs would splinter and split and merge together. I was already addicted to you, no such thing as too much of you, greedy I was, always wanting more. And then sleeping on your chest, your hands cradling my head, and deep, sleep-warmed kisses in the morning.

Do you remember when we went camping in Crianlarich? In the middle of a wood, our phones didn't work and we were perfectly, blissfully alone. The fires we made at night were so beautiful, bright flames that leapt and danced and warmed our faces and hands, even as the dark night slid its cold fingers down our collars. We drank whiskey straight from the bottle, we smoked a couple of joints, we listened to Neil Young crackling from your speakers, we talked for hours. When we went to bed our breathing was all we could hear, your skin so warm compared to the night. The fire had gone out, but we made our own heat. On the train home we were absolutely filthy, matted hair, dirty faces, black hands; three days in the woods had left dirt ingrained in the creases of our bodies. The first thing we did when we got home was get into the bath. Oh, it was lovely, clouds of steam and mountains of bubbles, and hot, hot water. You washed me so carefully, holding my arms and legs and soaping them clean, rubbing shampoo through my hair, a frown of concentration on your face.

Do you remember that time we played hide and seek in the dark? It was in your old bedroom, on Arlington Street. I hid on the top of the wardrobe. When you came into the room you hissed and snatched at the air, like a monster. I was already nervous, with that slightly hysterical excitement that comes with the game. I could hear your breathing, feel the air you were moving through rippling over my skin. There was laughter pressing tight against the top of my mouth, but I couldn't let it out because you'd find me. The longer you searched, the more nervous I became, and when your hands eventually grabbed my feet, a scream turned into helpless laughter. Of course, when you turned the lights back on I couldn't imagine how I'd managed to climb up on top of the wardrobe and couldn't see any way down. You suggested jumping from the wardrobe to the bed.
    'But I'll smash it into pieces!'
    'It's already half collapsed anyway, just jump!'
    Eventually you dragged over your desk and I jumped on to that, and then to the floor, where you caught me in your arms and said, 'Oh you're such a funny wee bug,' and I wriggled my hands like antennae and said, 'Not just any bug... a praying mantis!' And then I chased you round the room until we collapsed in a laughing heap on the bed, and it creaked and groaned like a ship in a storm.

Do you remember when you moved up north? You kept saying, 'But I'll see you on Friday,' with long, sweeping strokes of my back. You didn't understand how I felt; that you were leaving me behind, choosing your new job over me. When you left I shut the door and sat behind it, and cried and cried, a storm of tears, until I was half blind, my throat raw and my chest aching, the skin on my face and hands all swollen and tight from the salt. After a while the exhaustion that comes with that kind of crying settled over me, and I lay down on the couch and slept. When I woke it was dark. I went into the room that we'd been sharing for two months, and I walked around, picking up things that belonged to you, trying to find something that smelled of you. Eventually, I found a dirty T-shirt, so I lay down on the bed with it pressed to my face, and I looked out the window at the sodium-washed sky. I couldn't sleep that night, too small and alone in the big wide bed.

Do you remember when we were on holiday and we bought the Explorer? I remember sitting on the beach while you blew it up, almost the whole dinghy, with your mouth, and then I discovered in the box, along with the plastic oars, a pump. How we laughed! And then out on the waves of the Mediterranean, my hand trailing through the blue-green water and you rowing energetically and me singing. You rowed us round the headland, and we found a bit of rock to tie the Explorer to, and then we took off our swimming costumes and jumped into the water. And it felt so good against my naked skin, my instant new favourite thing, flowing over me seamlessly, and we too were seamless, rocking together in the sparkling ocean, every new moment washing over me with endless ripples of delight.

Do you remember that fight that we had in the bar on Portman Road? I was teasing you for falling asleep after dinner, and suddenly you turned, with angry eyes, and told me that I was a stupid little girl, that I didn't understand the stress you were under and how could I, when all I did was flit from my arty-farty course to my arty-farty job? I didn't know what having a real job was like. It's normal for people to be tired after working a full week, not that I'd know anything about that. I tried to point out that I'd had three jobs at the same time last year, but you laughed savagely and said, 'What, ushering, PRing and working as a shop girl? Oh what responsibility!'

'I worked long hours, and I was on my feet all day, not sitting in an office skiving on the Internet.'

'That's not what I do!'

'You told me that yourself.'

'Well, obviously I have other things to do. That's why they're paying me!'

'Well, I don't care! It's not my fault, you chose this job. It was you that chose to leave me and go up north for this job, so it's not my fault if you're tired!'

'Well it's nice to see you being so fucking supportive!'

I got up and lifted my coat and walked out on to Portman Square. I was crying, but pretending not to, trying to light a cigarette with shaking hands. After a couple of minutes you came out. You sighed and said, 'I'm sorry. Don't cry,' as you put your arms around me. I started crying in earnest then, gulping sobs into your shoulder as people around us stared. You said, 'I'm sorry. I'm just stressed. You have to be more understanding, darling.' I nodded mutely. You tilted my head up to your face with your hands, wiped away my tears, and said, 'Friends again?' I nodded again and we went back to the hotel.

Do you remember when you broke my heart? Things hadn't been good for a while, but I believed you when you said that you wanted to be with me forever. It was a hard night, a long night. We talked and talked, going round in circles. You told me why you weren't happy; I was too demanding, I expected too much from you, I was irrational and impulsive, I was too much for you. I listened, shocked, and tried to explain things, make excuses. But when you said, 'I've forgotten why I loved you', I knew it was over. Each one of those words was a punishment for everything I hadn't done for you, small but powerful fists that smacked me, one two three four five six times, in the gut. I don't remember feeling anything as you left. But I have spent so many days since then, missing you, my heart aching, my eyes darkened by unhappiness and a dull sadness settled over me, like a layer of ash. I remember you, your face, your body, your laugh, your smell, your warmth, your eyes, your skin, your smile, your voice. I cannot forget them.

Do you remember me?

Rab's beltin' story

Sean A McLaughlin

Right 'is wis it. Rab wis determined tae bi true tae ees ane language. He wis sick tae death a hivin tae write in ae Standard English. Thir wis nuhin *standard* aboot it. If Standard English wis so *standard* 'en why did naebody speak it? If it wis so *standard* 'en whit wis ae language thit wis comin oot o Rab's mooth? Sub-standard? Naw, Rab wisnae hivin 'at language fascism – ee'd nae time fur it, stuff 'at. He wis writin on ees ane terms noo. Nuhin wis goinae stop 'im.

He reflectid back on ees unorthodox muse.

'IT'S NO DOON; IT'S *DOWN*.' 'IT'S NO FLERR; IT'S *FLOOR*.' 'IT'S NO CLAES; IT'S *CLOTHES*. Christsake!' His maw hid shouted at 'im. 'YE SOUND LIKE YE'VE BEEN BLOODY DRAGGED UP. WHEN IR YE GOINAE LEARN TAE SPEAK RIGHT?'

'At wis ae conversation Rab hid hid wi ees maw on ees last visit. It hid been ae catalyst, ae blindin light, ae spur he needed.

'Maw, Ah love ye, but ye dae ma heid in,' wis Rab's partin shot, as he ran hame tae write his beltin' story.

It wisnae aw ees maw's inspiration, she couldnae take aw ae credit. He minded bein in ae primary classroom, where ae teacher used tae belt ye fur sayin 'aye' instead a 'yes': *Who do you think yer talkin to boy? Yer no wi yer pals noo, young man*. Even ae teacher couldnae keep up ae talkin in Standard English.

Rab reflected on aw they answers he knew in school but widnae put ees hand up fur. He wisnae sure thit he wid be able tae pull aff an acceptable accent in front o ae ees teachers. *Best tae shut up*, he thought at ae time. Efter aw anyhin's better thin slippin up and accidently drappin intae talkin like a bloody scruff: *I'm afraid I've dropped my pencil on the flerr, Miss*.

Scruff wis ae word used tae define Rab an his mates in 'em days. See NED hidnae been invented when Rab wis a wean. *Scrubber, scum, fish wife* (female vernacular speaker); aw these names wir attached tae ees accent when he wis a young yin.

Rab remembered ae nice young Modern Studies teacher in secondary.

'What you've got to understand class, is that there are certain ways of speaking in certain social situations.'

Noo although Rab liked 'er, he could see noo thit whit she wis really sayin wis, *'Noo whit ye've gottae realise guys, is thit as soon as ye open yer gub people ir goinae judge ye. If ye kin try an hide yer true accent then ye've git a better chance o gettin on.'* See, 'gettin on' wis whit it wis aw aboot.

Even ae careers officer used tae say, 'And how ir you going tae conduct yerself at the interview?'

'Ah doeno?' Rab sayd an shrugged ees teenage shoulders.

Rab knew even 'en, at 'at young age, thit if ye couldnae open yer mooth withoot gien yersell awae as scum then whit chance did ye hiv a gettin a *good* job?

'How'd ye expect tae get a good bloody job speakin' like 'at?' Ees maw hid constantly told 'im. She wis a total language fascist, Rab's maw, a loyal enemy foot soldier in ae battle tae SPEAK RIGHT! However, cause it wis Rab's maw he wid make sure thit 'at ae day o reckanin, when aw ae language killers wir roonded up – she'd get let aff. Well, it wis ees maw eftar aw.

Possibly kid on yer in a play, kid oan yer an actor. 'At hid accurred tae Rab when he eventually made it tae university. Thir wis a couple a people he knew thit hid jist wan day git aff ae train frae Port Glesga tae Glesga an changed their accent. They startid speakin in a sorta, West-end a glesga accent, only kinda wi a Edinburghy lilt. Rab wisnae sure if it worked completely, but it did seem thit they hid cleansed thirsells o their accent. Mibbae 'at wis whit aw them teachers an ees maw hid meant: Dae anyhin but whitever ae hell ye dae, don't open yer trap. Cause if ye dae? Ae games a boaggie.

But anough o ae past. Rab shook eesell. Noo Rab wis goinae put hings tae rights: 'Is book wis goinae change it aw.

Aw 'em Language Cleansers could noo kiss Rab's erse. He wis well an truly oot ae closet. A NED wi higher thought, proud tae be associated wi ae *Treggs* (yit another bloody name fur his kind).

Brothers an sisters, let us no gie a shite aboot whit people say aboot oor accent. Let us batter on bein' oorsells. Rab could see ae mobbed book signins.

Oh aye, an jist wait till ae telly came knockin. Melvin Bragg wid be invitin Rab on *The South Bank Show* in 'at guy on *The Culture Show* wid be fawnin. Rab knew his manifesto. He knew where he wis comin fae, he'd be ready fur 'em telly people.

'Ae revolution will no be subtitled, Melvin. Don't even hink aboot it. How ir ma brothers an sisters on ae lower west coast of Scotland ever goinae be understood if ye keep gien people subtitles? Ye promoted ae Liverpudlian accent in ae eighties, so ye kin dae it fur ma kind tae.' Oh aye, Rab wid show 'em.

Rab dragged eesell back frae his future stardom an git back doon tae ae matter in hand; bashin oot ae novel an legitimisin ae language. Thir wis nae time tae waste.

Thir wis wan thing Rab knew fur sure; he wis definitely hivin ae characters aw speakin in ae vernacular. Bit merr thin 'at, he wis also hivin ae third person narrator speakin in ae vernacular. Well why no? Ae way it always happend wis ae characters wid be free anough tae speak in an accent an dialect, but when it came tae any authorial voice at hid tae be in Standard English. Why? Wir they ae only voices o reason? Shite tae 'at.

God forbid thit a third person narrator hid an accent like Rab's! Think o ae confusion it wid cause wi ae critics: *I'm afraid I found it very hard to disassociate the voice of the narrator from that of the characters. The language gets in the way of the story. My brain can't handle a NED being the Godlike omniscient narrator AND speaking like the characters too. It's too much to comprehend!*

Well they wid jist hiv tae lump it 'is time, Rab thought. Oh aye, he wis definitely takin nae prisoners. If thir wis wan hing he wis goinae dae it wis be true tae 'is poor language, accent, dialect, vernacular, whit ever ae hell ye wanted tae call it. He wis goinae make sure 'is wee language o his wid shine. An why no? It wis as good as any wis it no? If people ir willin tae plough on through *Ulysses* 'en they kin plough oan through mine, he thought. An talkin a ploughs whit aboot auwl Rabbie Burns? Rab's namesake? Nae doubt people thought he wis an uneducated lower class shitkicker till somedae sayd different. *'It's no the language thit makes the man/ the man's the gowd...* right on, big man, Ah'm right way ye Rabbie, Rab thought.

Efter aw, when aw wis sayd an done did people no like new accents in their writin? Jesus, when Rab went tae university the students an lecturers wir trippin over thirsells tae discover ae new authentic, ethnic voice o Jamaica or Bangladesh or Bosnia. So why no Rab's Scots?

Aye, he wis definitely ontae somehin. Wis it no better tae hear a different voice fur wance? Oh aye, is wis goinae be a triumph for ae *West Mid Scots Vernacular,* ('at's whit ae university hid classified Rab's accent as). However, ees maw hid classified it as, *talkin like a bloody drunk on a street corner.*

But wait a minute. It accurred tae Rab thit probably people might be expectin tae see some well-worn, stock charactirs, like comedy drunks. He wisnae naïve enough no tae realise thit maist people wid begin bi projectin cultural stereotypes ontae ees language an novel. He could hear 'em: *Oh it seems to be a strand of Scots. Isn't it that Stanley Baxter skit, 'Parliamoglasgow'*? Mibbae ae audience wid be expectin some Gutter Realism; some drama aboot drunk Faithers an stuff. Mibbae they'd expect a wee touch o ae Billy Connelly aboot it? Well they could hink again. Because is wis goinae be a thought-provokin' masterpiece. People wid fall in love wi Rab's language, he'd be lauded, maybe even talked up as ae saviour of ae low land vernacular. Mibbae even bi known as startin a Movement – *The It'snoslang Movement.* Oh aye! 'Is wis it, ae realism o ae langauge wis ready tae be sprung on Rab's unsuspectin audience. Aw he needed tae dae noo wis think o a belter o a story.

Author biographies

Joe McInnes

Joe McInnes was born in Glasgow and has lived in London and Montreal. He graduated from Glasgow University in 2002 with an MA in Literature and went on to study creative writing at Strathclyde University before returning to Glasgow to enroll in the MLitt programme. He has had poetry published in *Cutting Teeth* and is currently working on a collection of short stories. He lists American authors Gerald Vizenor and Maxine Hong Kingston alongside Canadian novelist Thomas King as contemporary writers he admires. He has two teenage sons and a daughter in her early twenties.

Adrian Searle

Adrian Searle studied history and history of art at the University of Edinburgh and has worked in marketing, theatre and graphic design. His stories have been published in *The Herald*, *Latitude – An Anthology of New Writing from Scotland and The Philippines* (Anvil Press, 2005) and *The Research Club* (Black and White, 2007). He edited and published *The Hope That Kills Us – An Anthology of Scottish Football Fiction* (Freight, 2002) and *The Knuckle End – A Meaty Collection of New Scottish Writing* (Freight, 2005). He recently started a novel and lives in Glasgow with his partner and two children.

Roy McGregor

Roy McGregor was born and educated in Glasgow. He taught English and Drama full time in secondary schools and colleges for several years before moving to part-time work to concentrate on his writing. His book of plays for young people was published by Hodder Gibson in 2005 and he has edited a volume of contemporary plays for young people published by Hodder Gibson in 2007. A second volume of his own plays and screenplays will be published by Hodder Gibson at the end of 2008. He has written and published several short stories and is at the moment working on a novel.

Jenni Brooks

Jenni Brooks writes a variety of fiction, poetry and articles and has been published in the UK and Italy. She is currently working on her political play *Give a Man a Fish*. Jenni is a freelance youth worker, researcher and policy consultant working with a range of think-tanks and voluntary, community and campaigning organisations. She was previously an adviser to the Scottish government on civic participation and a member of the First Minister's Policy Unit. Born and bred in London, Jenni has spent time in many corners of the world and has been based in Scotland since 1995. She lives in Leith, Edinburgh.

Sue Reid Sexton

Sue Reid Sexton lives and works in Glasgow. When she's not writing she works as a counsellor specialising in trauma. She has written two novels about world war two. The first is about the greater mixing of social groups at that time and the unplanned pregnancies that resulted. The second covers the Clydebank blitz and the subsequent evacuation to the hut community at Carbeth. Both are concerned with belonging and loss. Continuing with timeless and therefore contemporary themes, she is currently working on a novel set in the present day about the connections between art, sex and bad parenting.

Celaen Chapman

Celaen Chapman was born in Birmingham in 1972 and moved to Scotland in 1993. Her first published short story appeared in the 2004 Scotsman and

Orange Short Story Award collection, *North – New Scottish Writing*, edited by Jackie Kay and published by Polygon. She also had a short story published in *Cleave: New Writing by Women in Scotland*, edited by Sharon Blackie and published by Two Ravens Press in the summer of 2008. She is currently working on a collection of short stories and a novel. She lives in Glasgow.

Patricia Ace

Patricia has had many poems and stories published in magazines and anthologies all over the UK including *Chapman, Edinburgh Review, The New Welsh Review, Honest Ulsterman, Envoi, Poetry Scotland, Haiku Scotland, Orbis* and *Northwords Now*. In 1995 Patricia was short-listed for the Christian Salvesen Robert Louis Stevenson Memorial Award. She has also won prizes in several poetry competitions, including the City of Cardiff International Poetry Competition, the Word's Out! Poetry Competition and the Litfest Poetry Competition. Patricia's chapbook collection, *First Blood*, was published by Happenstance Press in 2006. Most recently she had poems published in *Cleave: New Writing by Women in Scotland* from Two Ravens Press.

Fiona Rintoul

Fiona Rintoul is a journalist, editor and translator. She has published short stories and poems in *Mslexia, Poetry Scotland, The Research Club* and *The Hammicks Real Writers Anthology*. She has been short-listed for the Fish prose and poetry competitions and was a runner-up in the *Mslexia* 2006 Women's Poetry Competition. She is currently working on a novel set in Leipzig in the former East Germany where she studied for a time in the 1980s. In 2007, her novel-in-progress was short listed for the *Daily Telegraph's* Novel-in-a-Year Competition and in 2008 she won the first Gillian Purvis Award for New Writing. She lives in Glasgow.

Deborah Andrews

Deborah writes prose, poetry and drama. She is also co-founder and Artistic Director of Solar Bear, a Glasgow-based theatre company that produces innovative, multidisciplinary, inclusive work. In 1999 her theatrical adaptation of *Dream State: The New Scottish Poets* won a Scotsman

Fringe First. In 2004 she devised, scripted and directed *Seeing Voices*, winner of an Orange Community Futures Award and an Arts & Business Arts & Disability Award. In 2008 she was awarded RNID Champion of the Community. Deborah's short story UFO appears in the 2007 anthology *The Research Club*. She is currently drafting scenes for a novel.

Elinor Brown

Elinor Brown's short stories have been published in anthologies by Pulp Faction (*Allnighter*) and Egmont Press (*Love from Dad* and *Would you Believe It?*). She has written a collection of fables, is currently writing her first novel and also writes poetry in English and Italian. She works in drama development for film and television, most recently for the BBC and Janas Pictures (Sardinia), script reading and writing. She also reads fiction for Gallimard (Paris). She has worked as editor of several web sites for the BBC and pioneered the first exclusive antiquarian book dotcom. She researched the Radio 4 programmes *Lost, Stolen, Shredded* and *Rare Books, Rare People* and the spin-off book *Tolkien's Gown* by Rick Gekoski. Born in London, she spent several years living and writing in Sardinia and has recently moved to Glasgow.

JL Williams

JL Williams was born in New Jersey and studied at Wellesley College with the poet Frank Bidart. Her poetry has been published internationally in journals including *The New Writer*, *Barking Dogs*, laurahird.com, *Aesthetica*, *The Red Wheelbarrow*, *Chanticleer*, *The Wolf*, *Orbis*, *Fulcrum* and *Stand* (upcoming 2009). Since moving to Edinburgh in 2001 she has been active both as a poet and in the performing arts as a director and producer, most recently of the performance art cabaret Neue Liebe. She was recently awarded a grant from the Scottish Arts Council for a poetry collaboration entitled *chiaroscuro pentimenti* with composer Martin Parker and artist Anna Chapman.

Liam Murray Bell

Liam Murray Bell was born in the Orkney Islands, and continues to write about them, although he was brought up in Glasgow. After studying for an undergraduate degree at Queen's University Belfast, Liam returned to Glasgow to write for the MLitt in Creative Writing. He has been published in *New Writing Scotland* and his current project is a novel based in the village of St. Margaret's Hope, Orkney, in which a young beachcomber finds himself embroiled in a mysterious Trust that has led to both suicide and murder in the isolated and claustrophobic community.

EGJ

EGJ works as a freelance translator and writes somewhere between poetry and prose. EGJ has a Master of Letters in The Gothic Imagination from the University of Stirling and a Bachelor of Arts in English from Lund University. Texts have appeared in a number of anthologies, *Ponton, Serum, Frostwriting, Bard, The Turnip* and *From Glasgow to Saturn,* and are forthcoming in *The Clockwise Cat* and *The Recusant.* Born just outside Malmö, Sweden EGJ lives around Stirlingshire, Scotland.

CJ Begg

Not yet old but no longer young, CJ Begg is from Ayrshire; was educated at Glasgow University and University of Technology, Sydney, and works in the booming mass healthcare industry of the West of Scotland. He spent several years on the sunny side of the world, but returned to Glasgow for the weather and to start an MLitt on the University's acclaimed creative writing programme. This is his first published short story. He is currently writing a novel and a radio comedy script.

Margaret Callaghan

Margaret Callaghan left a career as a policy adviser at the treasury to study for the creative writing MLitt at the University of Glasgow. She has had light-hearted articles published in *The Herald* and the *Scotsman* and has been runner up in short story competitions. In her writing, Margaret is interested in how people become the person that they are, how they are perceived by different people, and what they don't say. Margaret has just finished her first novel which is about three friends growing up in Glasgow and London in the 1980s, 1990s and 2000s.

Ulrich Hansen

Originally from Denmark, Ulrich is now living in Scotland. Having graduated from Glasgow University with an English Literature degree in 2000, the Creative Writing MLitt is his first serious venture into writing. Up until now his preferred form has been very short prose. Often those pieces are sparked off by other literature, films and TV, things heard on the bus. Apart from the piece in this anthology, some of his shorter fiction will be included in a forthcoming collection, published by Ziji Publishing. He is currently working on his first novel.

Sue Wilson

Born in London to Glaswegian parents, Sue Wilson grew up in Sussex and Cambridgeshire before attending Edinburgh University, and has lived in the Scottish capital ever since. As a freelance arts journalist, she has written for a wide range of publications including the *Scotsman*, the *Independent*, the *Sunday Herald*, the *List*, *Scotland on Sunday* and *Songlines* magazine, and is co-author of *The Rough Guide to Irish Music* (2001). 'Bona fides' is one of several short stories she has written while studying part-time for the Glasgow MLitt and she is also currently working on a novel.

Lucy Adams

Lucy Adams is Chief Reporter at *The Herald* newspaper. Born in Yorkshire, she has worked in Scotland as a journalist for the past nine years and spent four years at *The Sunday Times* in Glasgow covering education and home affairs. In 2007 she won both the Amnesty International UK and Scottish Nations and Regions media award for her coverage of post civil war Liberia. In 2008 she won a One World Media Award for her coverage of communities in Northern Uganda. She lives in Glasgow with her boyfriend. Hobbies include mountaineering and cycling.

Fiona Montgomery

Fiona Montgomery lives near Glasgow. She has worked for Scottish CND, was a reporter and political reporter for the *Evening Times* in Glasgow, has taught news reporting at Napier University and was Information &

Resource Worker with Rape Crisis Scotland. She works now in policy and information at UNISON Scotland. In the early 1990s Fiona was part of the launch collective for the Scottish feminist magazine *Harpies & Quines*. She dabbles in poetry and loves journalism, creative non-fiction and memoir. This is her first published short story. She may eventually tackle a novel. She is married, with two daughters and two grand-daughters.

EJ Patience

EJ Patience has won various prizes in Scottish Association of Writers competitions, has had poetry and short stories published and has written for the e-zine *From Glasgow to Saturn*. She has also written for Radio 4 and is currently working on her first novel. She describes her work as somewhat bi-polar, being drawn to write about the darker side of human nature, but also finds herself writing humorous prose with equal enthusiasm. Originally from Edinburgh, she studied in Aberdeen and became a librarian working within the oil industry, education system and National Health Service. She lived in various parts of Scotland before settling in East Dunbartonshire where she now lives with her family and animals.

A Singerman

Alexander William Singerman was born in Yorkhill Hospital in Glasgow on 19 June 1985. He is the son of a solicitor and a history teacher. He read American Studies at the University of Edinburgh and the University of California, San Diego. He has spent much of his life waiting on tables in Di Maggios' resturants in Glasgow and the rest writing in various ways.

Helen Sedgwick

Helen Sedgwick was born and grew up in London. She moved to Edinburgh at the turn of the millennium to pursue a career in physics, which she followed to Glasgow in 2005. Discovering that she wanted to write, she began the University of Glasgow's MLitt in Creative Writing in October 2007, and is one of the editors of the MLitt's on-line magazine, *From Glasgow to Saturn*. Her scientific writing has been published in journals ranging from *Nature* to the *European Physical Journal* and she is currently writing her first novel.

Susan Kemp

For the last ten years Susan has been producing and directing factual programmes for the BBC. Her most recent successes include *Reported Scotland*, a 50-year history of news on television and *Deadline*, the warts and all story of the Scottish Press. Prior to her television career Susan worked in the low budget/no budget film world, scraping a few pennies together and blagging her way to telling stories on film. She produced the award-winning short film *Pan-Fried* and wrote and directed *Hill of Beans*. She now feels ready for the challenge of telling stories without pictures.

William Gault Bonar

William Gault Bonar was born in Greenock in 1953 and grew up in the neighbouring town of Port Glasgow. He left home for Edinburgh in 1972 and later attended the University of Edinburgh graduating with honours in English Language and Literature in 1981. His many places of employment have included shipyards, libraries, factories, hospitals, schools, pubs and oil rigs. He is a former teacher of English and now an Educational Psychologist. His first poetry pamphlet, *Frostburn Steel*, appeared in 2004. He also publishes the poetry of others under the imprint Dreadful Night Press.

Mary Paulson-Ellis

Mary Paulson-Ellis is variously a writer, mother, fundraiser, administrator, chaperone, reviewer and tutor. In 2006 she received a Scottish Arts Council New Writers Bursary and was published in *Making Soup in a Storm, New Writing Scotland 24* (ASLS). In 2007 she was short-listed for the *Daily Telegraph*'s Novel-in-a-Year competition and commended in the New Writing Partnership's New Writing Ventures competition. In August 2007, she was published in *The Research Club* (CHROMA), an anthology of work by Glasgow University students, competitively selected by two writers, an agent and a literary editor. She is currently writing a novel.

Kirsty Logan

Kirsty Logan was born in 1984. She lives in the south side of Glasgow. She started out writing novels, but is now concentrating on short stories and screenplays. One script, *Tracks*, was recently made into a short film. Kirsty graduated from the University of Stirling in 2006 with a degree in English Literature. She has worked in a variety of jobs, the most enjoyable of which was as a children's bookseller. She enjoys travelling and her favourite destinations are Krakow, Venice and Cape Town. She hopes to continue these travels – dream destinations include Wellington, Toronto and Grand Bahama.'

Kate Tough

Kate Tough has had many short stories, flash fictions and poems published in the UK and Canada. Her story, 'Slight Catch', is an adapted extract from her novel-in-progress. In addition to writing, Kate has worked on short film scripts, film reviews and recorded and produced a radio series in Canada. She has read her work at events, including the Wigtown Book Festival – where she was also a 'Book Doctor', offering first aid to lay writers. Kate enjoys working with adults and children in a creative capacity and currently facilitates writing workshops in community settings.

Amy Burns

Amy Burns is originally from Birmingham, Alabama, but makes her home in Scotland. Her prose and poetry has been published both on-line and in print. She has worked as an editor/publisher of the literary journal *Unbound Press* and as a ghost writer of a now published novel. Although, to date, her publications have predominately been short fiction, she has completed her first novel, an innovative co-written project, and she is now working on her second novel.

Alison Sommerville

Alison Sommerville has always been interested in writing. This interest has involved facilitating community writing groups, working in the field of adult literacy and now pursuing her own work. She grew up in Canada and Australia before moving to Scotland in 1991 where she lives with a house full of boys (one husband and three sons).

Barry Gornell

Barry Gornell, a Liverpool born ex- firefighter, lives on the west coast of Scotland where he is trying to grow up with his children. He is supported in this by his wife. His writing career started with a BBC Opening Shots commission in 1996, followed by the acclaimed short film, *Sonny's Pride* (1998). *The Race* (2004), his second film, was shot on the island of Barra, where his preoccupations – landscape, isolation, family and the weakness in men who want to be strong – converge. He is corralling a themed collection of short stories and is in the early stages with three novels.

Jénnifer Ádcock

Jénnifer Ádcock was born in Mexico in 1982. She majored in Hispanic Literature at ITESM, where she met Mexican novelist Felipe Montes and worked as his research assistant. With other students under Montes' tutelage, they founded the Fábrica Literaria for taking and facilitating writing workshops. She was awarded a grant by the Writers' Center of Nuevo León in 2006 and was runner-up in *Caza de Letras,* a national online writing competition organized by the UNAM. She has worked as a translator, puppeteer and English teacher and is a member of the experimental folk band Kelvin's Autumnal Thundercunt. She relocated to Glasgow in 2007.

Lucy West

Lucy West was born in Glasgow in 1983 but was brought up in the new town of East Kilbride. She completed a degree in English Literature at the University of Glasgow in 2005 before spending a brief period working and living in London. She writes short stories and has been working on a longer piece, which she hopes will one day become a novel. She plans to try her hand at children's fiction next.

Jessica Parkinson

Jessica was born in Malawi and brought up in Canada. She studied International Development and Women's Studies in Peterborough, Ontario. She has lived in such places as Ghana and Penghu, and has travelled overland from Hong Kong to Poland. She has settled in Kilcreggan on the west coast of Scotland. She lives in a house that has been in her family for five generations and had been uninhabited for ten years. When not absorbed in this restoration project, Jessica writes stories and poems. She draws on her travel experience and her search for home for inspiration.

Joyce Henderson

Joyce Henderson spent her childhood in rural Fife. After four years studying in Edinburgh, she moved to London to work in public relations, then spent 13 years working her way back to Scotland. Life took a strange turn when she fell in with the Buddhists, renounced PR and was given a Sanskrit name. Her writing is an attempt to invent something even weirder than her life, but sometimes it's just her life thinly disguised. This is her first published short story.

Maria Di Mario

Maria Di Mario was born and brought up in Glasgow. She studied Italian and English Literature at Glasgow University, spending a year in Rome as part of her degree. After graduating in 2007, she took up a place on the MLitt in Creative Writing course. This is her first published story. She lives in the west end of Glasgow and is in the process of writing her first novel.

Sean A McLaughlan

Sean McLaughlan, an English/Media Studies teacher by day, has been writing for years in his Port Glasgow vernacular. A short story writer, he has been published in a number of magazines and anthologies. At present he is working on a collection of short stories, *Tales fae ae Orchard* set in and around a fictitional Port Glasgow.